Something about the man standing on the sidewalk was familiar.

He fit his blue jeans nicely though they were faded, ripped and soiled in a few spots. Regardless, he looked like he was hewn out of solid rock. Well over six feet, and all torso, the man had a narrow waist and a tight, high butt. His T-shirt, though relatively clean, adhered like a Band-Aid across his broad chest and wide shoulders. The sleeves rolled up to reveal corded forearms. Aviator dark glasses, the kind in vogue, hid his eyes.

He must have noticed her staring because he inclined his head but did not smile.

“Glad you made it home safely from church,” he said. “My great-grandmother, Belle Carter, sends your grandmother her regards.”

Derek Morse, a completely different-looking man than the one who’d been to church yesterday in his professional gray suit. He’d helped Gran into her car.

“What are you doing here?” Joya asked, aware her voice sounded a little too high.

Books by Marcia King-Gamble

Kimani Romance

Flamingo Place
All About Me
Down and Out in Flamingo Beach

Kimani Press Sepia

Jade
This Way Home
Shattered Images

Kimani Press Arabesque

Remembrance
Eden's Dream
Under Your Spell
Illusions of Love
A Reason To Love
Change of Heart
Come Fall
Come Back to Me
A Taste of Paradise
Designed for You

MARCIA KING-GAMBLE

fell in love with the romance genre after reading her first Mills and Boon book at age six. When she grew up, she freelance read for Harlequin and Silhouette Books, earned degrees in psychology and theater, and she worked as an executive in the travel industry. And after reading every plot possible, she decided writing romances was what she wanted to do. Her first romance was published in 1998.

Eight years later, with eighteen novels and two novellas under her belt, Marcia continues to write for both the romance and women's fiction market. She now writes for several Harlequin imprints. Marcia's books are national bestsellers, and she's been nominated for numerous awards. Marcia currently lives in south Florida.

DOWN AND OUT IN FLAMINGO *Beach*

MARCIA KING-GAMBLE

With grateful thanks to my agent Amy Moore Benson.
Let's hope the third one's a charm.

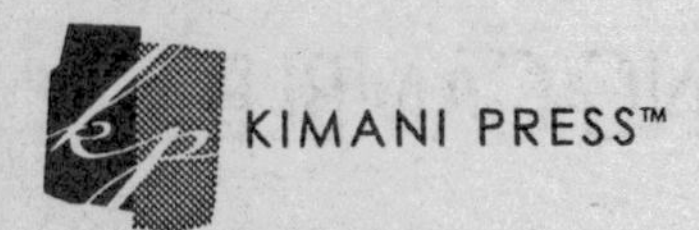

ISBN-13: 978-0-373-86016-6
ISBN-10: 0-373-86016-1

DOWN AND OUT IN FLAMINGO BEACH

www.kimanipress.com

Printed in U.S.A.

Dear Reader,

Down and Out in Flamingo Beach is the third title in my FLAMINGO BEACH miniseries. Previous titles in the series include *Flamingo Place,* my first Kimani Romance title and *All About Me.* Like many quaint beach communities, Flamingo Beach continues to change and grow.

In this the third book of the series, the north Florida town of Flamingo Beach is celebrating its 100-year anniversary along with Nana Belle, the oldest living resident on the beach. I hope you were able to attend her party.

On a personal note, I have always loved small beachfront communities that remind me of a time when life was simple. I'd take them any day over the more glitzy upscale resorts. But times are changing, and nothing lasts forever. Do we change along with the times or do we risk becoming dinosaurs?

That is exactly the message of this story. An open mind leaves us open to possibilities. Change, though unsettling, can be good and often what we think we want is not what we need. So get out that strict list of must-haves and deal-breakers and give them another look. With a little adjustment you just might find that perfect love.

Romantically yours,

Marcia King-Gamble

Chapter 1

"So what do you think about Quen getting married?" the woman asked, her eyes never leaving Joya's face.

Her ex-husband's wedding was not something Joya Hamill wished to discuss with a stranger. But the question had come out of left field, catching her totally off guard.

The woman had come up to her and her grandmother unexpectedly as they'd emerged from Flamingo Beach Baptist Church. The congregation of mostly African-Americans dressed in their Sunday finery stood catching up on town gossip. Joya had been gazing at the women in their elegant wide-brimmed hats, stylish suits and hose, even though the temperature was well in the eighties, when the woman had swooped down.

Gathering out front was an after-service routine. Many came to church to see, be seen and catch up on Flamingo Beach's gossip. Later that afternoon these same people would be eating their lavish Sunday dinner while discussing the outfits and speculating on who was doing who. Everyone was fair game, and if you weren't up to snuff, guaranteed you would be trashed. As a result, the one Black-owned beauty shop in town did a thriving business on Saturday afternoons after paychecks were cashed.

When the church woman had first approached, Joya had thought she might be collecting for some charity, but she'd soon discovered that it was gossip she was after.

"And to Chere Adams at that," the woman continued. "I would have thought he'd would have gone for someone slimmer."

Mind you, the church lady was no lightweight herself. Now how to respond diplomatically without being rude? Not that she didn't deserve to be put in her place, but Flamingo Beach was a small town and it didn't pay to make enemies.

Joya let the warm Florida sunshine play over her

cheeks. She tilted her head back, letting a balmy breeze ruffle her ponytail. She'd felt especially uplifted, even though it had been a lengthy Baptist service and the clapboard church had been warm and stuffy. She was a Catholic and used to a more somber mass. But she'd enjoyed the sermon because it was livelier than she was used to and the congregation took part. Joya had only gone because Granny J with her fractured ankle needed someone to drive her. And Joya just couldn't say no to Granny.

Joya continued looking around her. Granny J was engrossed in conversation with a customer who'd bought one of her quilts and didn't know how to launder it. But Joya knew she was still tuned into this conversation. The old lady's hearing was sharper than that of most people half her age. At seventy-five she didn't miss a thing.

"You must feel awful," the woman persisted, her eyes darting over to the area where Quen Abrahams, Joya's ex-husband, and his fiancée, Chere, were chatting with Jen St. George and her radio-personality husband, with whom she'd eloped. The two had scrapped an elaborate wedding and gone on a cruise. They'd gotten married at one of the ports of call.

"If you'll excuse me, I need to take my grandmother home," Joya said, attempting to walk away.

The woman made no attempt to move. She leaned

in as if exchanging confidences, "Everyone knows that woman is Ian Pendergrass's ho."

Joya needed to put a stop to it *now.* She wasn't happy that Quen was remarrying, but not for the reasons most people thought. Quen getting married again was a reminder of just how single and without viable prospects she was. Flamingo Beach did not have the types of men Joya wanted. It was much too laid-back and too provincial. The moment Granny J's ankle healed and she was given a clean bill of health, Joya was out of here.

"I need to get off my feet, hon," Granny J said, breaking into the conversation. Her grandmother linked an arm through hers. "You'll have to excuse us, dear."

Granny J's fractured ankle in its soft cast was mending just fine. Yesterday she'd been out and about shopping for hours. Joya knew that the grandmother she'd been named after was just trying to get her out of an awkward and insensitive situation.

"We do have to leave," Joya said diplomatically. "Will I see you at Quen and Chere's wedding?"

Looking visibly deflated, the churchwoman sputtered, "You're invited? You couldn't possibly be thinking of attending?"

Granny J, sensing Joya was about to lose it, tugged on her arm. "Honey, we really must go, my ankle is beginning to throb."

Joya wished the woman a nice day, and she and Granny J walked away. Out of earshot she said, "Thank you, Gran, for saving the day. I was one step away from cussing her out."

"Not even worth it." Granny continued smiling and nodding at the people she knew, which was everyone. They picked their way through the crowd, heading toward a Lincoln Continental parked in the handicapped spot. The car was way too big and Joya hated it, but Granny J preferred a lot of padding around her.

"Just in case my reflexes fail me, dear and I get into an accident."

Both Joya and Granny J were petite—maybe five feet two inches on a good day. Joya always wore heels and Granny J had a good fifty pounds on Joya. The younger woman had a milk-chocolate complexion. Her grandmother's was a smidgen darker. They both had gray eyes. Because of weight and the fractured ankle, Granny was a little slower in gait. She'd refused to use the cane the doctor had given her, stating, "Only old geezers use canes, and I am not an old geezer."

Truthfully, nothing was wrong with Granny's faculties. She could remember the history behind every quilt she'd ever made. Her memory went way back, and her unlined face made people who didn't know her believe she was at least a decade younger.

Joya depressed the remote button on the car's key chain. She was trying to hold the door open with one hip, and settle Granny J in the front when a deep male voice came from behind her.

"Hey, be happy to help you ladies."

Joya turned to see a towering, dark-complexioned man standing behind her. Though he looked as though he might be hewn from a rock, he was dressed in a gray suit, white shirt and red tie. He looked powerful. Joya surmised that he too had attended the church service. How come she hadn't seen him inside?

Yes, the church was packed, and they'd been seated in the pew up front that the Hamills had paid dues on for years…still…

Joya smiled at the man. "Thanks, that would really be appreciated." She relinquished the car door to his care.

His answering smile was a flash of white against ebony. His skin was smooth as velvet and his eyes were the color of toffee. His cheekbones were two slashes on the sides of his face, and his nostrils flared slightly. He was what her grandmother would call a hunk. She thought he was hot. Sizzling.

He held the door and waited until Granny J got settled, then in an easy movement he went around to the driver's side and held the door for Joya.

"Thanks, Derek," Granny J said twiddling her fingers at him. "Be sure to give my best to Belle."

"Thank you," Joya added after she'd slid into the driver's seat. She caught his smile and realized how ridiculous she must look sitting on one of Granny's quilted pillows so that her feet could reach the pedals.

Derek, whatever his last name was, stood back watching them. Joya made sure Granny J had her seat belt on—the old lady had a tendency not to wear it—before starting up the car.

She waved to the Derek person and thanked him again.

"Step on it," Granny J ordered. "I have quilting to do."

Joya carefully backed out of the handicapped spot.

"Am I suppose to know Derek?" she asked as they headed back to Granny J's Craftsman-style home which also served as her shop.

"He's Belle Carter's great-grandson. His name is Derek Morse."

Joya knew who Belle was. Everyone in Flamingo Beach knew the almost centenarian. She was going to be the same age as the town, and although she could no longer walk, her memory was right up there with Granny J's.

"Hmmm," Joya said, keeping her eye on the road,

"I didn't know your friend Belle had grandsons that were professionals."

Granny J said nothing. Joya could tell her mind had returned to the quilt she was working on. Her grandmother lived to make quilts and she was always designing one quilt or another in her head. She'd taught Joya the skill when she was very young. While most kids were out playing, Joya sat in Granny J's shop brainstorming one Afrocentric pattern after another while listening to the history of the roles African-American women played in quilt-making and design.

They were on Flamingo Row now, otherwise known as The Row. It was where Granny J had always lived. Now it was considered the historical district and more and more stores were opening up. The narrow tree-lined streets had mostly Craftsman-style homes. Several of the owners lived in the back rooms or in separate buildings behind their shops. Flamingo Row was the street the town had been created around.

Joya parked the car at the side entrance and came around to help Granny J out.

"You'll be back for dinner," the older woman said, making it more a statement than a question.

"Of course I will. You know I never pass up a roast."

She escorted the old lady inside and helped her out

of her church clothes and into a comfortable cotton shift. Granny stuck one foot into a sneaker, poured herself a beer—a Sunday indulgence—grabbed a brown-paper bag of pork rinds, and took a seat in front of her big-screen TV with the remote. She picked up the quilt she'd been working on and examined it closely.

"I just don't get why someone as homely as Elda would want to put her mug on this." She was referring to the fact that her customer had insisted on having her features on every other block of the quilt. Granny had tried to dissuade her but Elda was the customer, and paying big money at that, so Granny had dutifully had the image transferred to the material as she'd wanted.

"I'll see you at four," Joya said letting herself out.

She drove the Lincoln Continental across town, struggling to keep the huge automobile on the road and hating every minute of it. She much preferred her compact BMW convertible. In it she felt pretty and carefree. In the Lincoln she just felt old. She was thirty-three although she'd been told she barely looked twenty-one. Still she was getting up there, and if she was going to make any real money, she needed to do something about an alternative career, things being what they were with the airlines these days. Right before leaving L.A., she'd enrolled in an interior-design class. But she'd put that on hold.

Joya passed a number of buildings under construction. The land developers, realizing there was only so much available waterfront left in North Florida, were building purely on speculation. Every day more and more people were moving in, since housing on Flamingo Beach was still relatively inexpensive.

She pulled into the newly gated community of Flamingo Place, and navigated the spacious sedan into the covered parking space that came with her condo. Some people might think it strange that she lived in the same complex as her ex and his soon-to-be wife, even rented one of his apartments, but the truth of the matter was that they got along well now that they were divorced, and she and Chere had become quite good friends.

Joya would actually miss them when she went back to L.A. and returned to the flight-attendant job from which she'd taken an extended leave of absence. L.A. International was already applying the pressure, sending her letters hoping she would come back.

Well, she planned on doing just that as soon as Granny was able to stand firmly on both feet. Joya passed on the elevator, ignoring the blisters at the back of her heels. She skipped up the stairs to her third-floor apartment. Walking, even walking in heels that were beginning to pinch, helped keep her trim.

Joya had left the air conditioning running and it felt pleasantly cool in the two-bedroom apartment. Anxious to get comfortable, she began stripping off clothes at the door. That was one of the beautiful things about living alone. You didn't have to stand on ceremony for anybody. She was down to thong panties and her bra when the phone rang.

At first she was not going to pick up, anyone who knew her well would have her cell-phone number. But the ringing persisted and something told her she'd better get it.

"Joya Hamill?" The voice sounded official. Serious.

"Yes, this is she."

"This is Officer Greg Santana."

Officer. Police. Greg Santana. They'd gone to high school together. Joya squeezed her eyes shut. It wouldn't be good news. She could feel it. And although she'd been very young, she remembered another call that had changed her life; both her parents and her two brothers had died in a car accident one fateful night, casualties of a drunk driver. Granny J was now all she had left.

"Joya, are you there?"

"I'm here, Greg."

"I'm calling about Mrs. Hamill, Granny J."

A vise settled around Joya's chest. She had difficulty breathing. "What about Mrs. Hamill?"

"She's been taken to the hospital by ambulance. She asked that I call you."

"But how could that be? I just left her."

"She called 911 a few minutes ago. An ambulance was dispatched."

Joya got the particulars from Greg, grabbed the first pair of shorts she could find and slipped a sleeveless top over her head. She shoved her feet into flip-flops, grabbed the car keys and took the three flights of steps two at a time.

When Joya got to Flamingo Beach General she had to fight with one of those overly cheery nurses to see Granny J, but at least the elderly woman wasn't in intensive care. The nurse told her Granny had experienced chest pains and knew enough to get the medics out. Doctor Benjamin, who was on duty, suspected indigestion. He'd ordered a series of tests and the decision had been made to keep Granny J overnight for observation. Now the old lady was resting comfortably.

It took a full three hours before Joya was allowed to see her grandmother. The round little woman was lost amongst plump white pillows. So many tubes were attached to her arms she looked like a marionette and it was hard to say where she started and they ended.

"Five minutes," the nurse said. "And only because you insisted you wait."

"Is Granny's doctor on duty?" Joya asked. She wanted to speak to the doctor and make sure she felt comfortable with him. She wanted to tell him that this was not the first time her grandmother had experienced chest pains. They usually came on after her Sunday beer, which she drank while snacking on pork rinds.

"Dr. Benjamin has left for the day," the nurse answered with some finality. "It's been a long shift."

"You should have gotten here earlier and you would have met him," Granny J called from somewhere in the bed sheets. She sounded healthy as an ox. "That Dr. Ben is worth meeting. Know if he's married?" she asked the nurse.

"He has a girlfriend."

Granny J snorted. "Girlfriends are easily gotten rid of. If you want him, Joya I'll set something up."

Joya pretended to glare at her grandmother, though a doctor did sound good. But Granny J hardly sounded as though she was dying so she exhaled a huge sigh of relief.

"How long before she can come home?" Joya asked the nurse, who was trying to smother a smile.

"That depends on Dr. Benjamin. He'll want to see the test results, and depending on what he finds it could be as early as tomorrow."

"Do you need anything, Gran?" Joya asked, realizing the sun was beginning to set.

"Just my quilting. They wouldn't let me take Elda Carson's work with me in the ambulance."

"And a good thing, too. If you're not released by tomorrow. I'll bring it to you."

"Yes, please, and come around the time Dr. Ben is doing his rounds. I'll need you to open the shop. We open at nine promptly."

"Yes, I know," Joya said, rolling her eyes, and then she and the nurse exchanged conspiratorial looks. She had the feeling Granny J would be just fine. She had to be. Granny dying or infirm wasn't something she wanted to think about.

Chapter 2

A little before nine the next morning, Joya parked Granny J's car in the alley reserved for the shopkeepers. She found the house keys in the usual place, under the pot of geraniums on the porch, and let herself in through the side door.

The keys to the shop were exactly where Granny had said she would find them, hanging on a nail in the back of the closet. Joya tucked them in her purse and opened the windows to let the balmy ocean breeze in. Granny J did not believe in air conditioning.

Joya walked into the store, using the door separating the house from the shop. It never ceased to amaze her that the place was the same as she remembered it as a child. Nothing had really changed except for the peeling paint on the wall.

With a practiced eye, Joya looked around the four rooms that made up the store. The back room, originally a combined kitchen and dining area, was where the quilt guild—beginners to more advanced—met twice a week to develop their skills and work on their comforters. Occasionally the ladies sponsored public quilt shows to raise money for charitable causes.

This same room held a large oak table surrounded by stiff wooden chairs. In the corner were two comfortable Queen Anne seats. Sewing machines were all grouped in one spot, and everywhere the tools of the trade were visible. Reed baskets held thimbles, scissors, scraps of material and itsy-bitsy quilting needles that were called betweens.

The small cubicle was where Granny J had her office. On the other side of that room was a huge storage closet where she kept her fabric and batting.

What the general public saw was the big showroom up front with the enclosed porch facing the street. It was large and sunny with a slanted wooden floor. The walls here were in sad need of a fresh coat of paint.

Outside noises intruded as more and more storekeepers opened for the day. Gran's neighbors were, for the most part, a friendly bunch and everyone looked out for the others.

Joya made herself focus. What would she do if she were given leeway to perk the place up? Right now it reminded her of some crazy bazaar with jumbled bits of cloth everywhere. Most of the quilts were hard to see. And yes, some colorful tapestries hung from the walls, but the more expensive were folded in smudged display cabinets that could use a good polishing. Afrocentric patterns were hidden from the eye because of the way they were folded. Story quilts were displayed alongside more traditional quilts. The whole place was a mess.

Thrown on a huge brass bed that needed polishing were mosaic patchwork quilts, their hexagons sewn together to form intricate designs. Next to them were comforters depicting historical and biblical events, a style made famous by the nineteenth-century African-American quilt maker, Harriet Powers of Athens.

What Granny's place needed was order. Order and a big sprucing-up.

The store had huge rectangular windows that looked right out on Flamingo Row. The seats below them held more quilts and rows of patchwork cushions. Newer patterns like Double Wedding Ring, Dresden Plate and Little Dutch Girl resided here.

Granny J had once told Joya this was a deliberate strategy to catch the eye of passersby looking for attractive souvenirs but who didn't want to spend lots of money.

If this were Joya's shop she'd decorate it differently. Who said a quilt shop had to look like a little old lady owned it? It would have nice warm peach walls and the brass bed would be angled in a more inviting manner. She'd get rid of all that clutter. And she'd cover the bed with the most attractive and expensive quilt in the place, which of course would change on a weekly basis. There'd be flowers and scented candles everywhere. Who knew, she might even offer pedicures or foot massages. Relaxed women spent money.

A tapping on the front door got her attention.

"Anyone home?" a man's voice called.

"Just me."

Joya had completely forgotten about flipping the Closed sign in the window to Open.

She pushed open the front door and stuck her head out.

"Hi, Chet!"

Chet Rabinowitz, the mayor's son, and part owner of All About Flowers took a step back, gaping at her. "Where's Granny J?" He seemed surprised to see Joya.

"In the hospital. Kept overnight until test results come back."

Chet clutched his heart, "Oh, my God. Tell me it's nothing serious. Harley," he shrieked to his partner and lover. "Granny J's in the hospital. We need to send her the biggest arrangement we have."

Harley Mancini, Chet's partner, came running, clutching the sunflowers he'd been arranging in an oversized vase. "Did you say something happened to Granny J?"

Joya explained what had happened and reassured them her granny would be fine. At least she hoped so. She'd called the hospital right before leaving the condo and the nurse had told her Granny J was resting comfortably.

"Will you be running the shop for her then?" Chet quizzed, giving Joya a dubious look as if that couldn't possibly be happening. Chet had made it clear from the very first time they'd met that he thought she was all fluff and a general waste of time. And truthfully, Joya had made no effort to charm him. She wasn't that crazy about Chet. She'd pegged him a busybody and much preferred Harley. He was by far the more diplomatic of the two.

Without waiting to be invited in, Chet sashayed by her. He scrunched up his nose and sniffed loudly. "Joya's Quilts needs help. It even smells old."

"Chet," Harley admonished, "Be nice!"

"I am *always* nice. Nice and honest."

"It's way after nine, how come the two Ms. Things aren't here? Or are they eating? They eat all the time." Chet poked his head into the guild room and shook his head. "Late again. What a waste of time those two are."

Joya had almost forgotten about the two women Granny J employed. She made a mental note to look for LaTisha and Deborah's phone numbers in the Rolodex Granny J still used. She'd give them a call.

A loud banging came from the other side of the partition. Joya frowned but Chet wiggled his head knowingly. "Hallelujah. Construction has begun."

"Construction?" Joya repeated. "Is one of the stores being renovated?"

"*We* are being renovated," he announced, arms wide to encompass the block. "The two buildings on either side of you and those across the street have started. I can't wait to have my grand reopening."

If the entire block was getting a facelift, why wasn't Joya's Quilts? This was something she'd take up with her grandmother.

Joya addressed Harley, who'd been very quiet. "Where's this money coming from?"

"The bank," Chet answered. "There are special low-interest loans being offered to store owners, all because of the hundred-year anniversary of Flamingo Beach. This centennial will bring tourists here in droves. We're in the Historical District. This is where Flamingo Beach got started and that's why we're being showcased."

Why hadn't Joya heard about this gentrification before? Because she'd been trying to deal with the fact that her ex was moving on.

"How did you find out about these loans?" Joya asked, "And why hasn't Granny applied for one?" It was a rhetorical question. She already knew the answer.

"Remember who Chet's daddy is?" Harley added, smiling and winking at her.

"Did you explain to my grandmother how they work?" Joya persisted, looking from one man to the other.

"Yup. But she didn't want to deal with the paperwork, though I offered to help." Chet leaned in and placed his hands on his hips. "You know your grandmother and how stubborn she is. She told me her store looks fine just the way it is. She doesn't need any showpiece."

It sounded like something Granny J would say. She was practical to the bone.

"Excuse me." Another man's voice came from the road. "If that's your SUV you'll need to move it."

"Hang on, Derek. Be right back," Chet's partner called, racing off to move the truck he'd parked illegally while unloading it.

Vehicles were technically not allowed on the narrow cobblestoned streets of Flamingo Row. It was supposed to be a pedestrian haven, allowing shoppers to roam freely and safely in and out of stores.

Something about the man standing on the sidewalk was familiar. He fitted his blue jeans nicely, though they were faded, ripped and soiled in a few spots. He was well over six feet with a narrow waist and a tight high butt. His T-shirt, though relatively clean, adhered like a bandage across his broad chest and wide shoulders. The sleeves rolled up to reveal corded forearms. Aviator-style sunglasses, the kind in vogue, hid his eyes.

He must have noticed her staring because he inclined his head but did not smile.

"Glad you made it home safely from church," he said. "My great-grandmother, Belle Carter, sends your grandmother her regards."

It was Derek Morse, a completely different-looking man than the one who'd been to church yesterday in his professional gray suit. He'd been the one who'd helped Gran into her car.

"What are you doing here?" Joya asked, aware her voice sounded a little too high. She'd almost forgotten about Chet, who stood checking them out but for once wasn't running his mouth. That would come later.

"Working," Derek answered.

"Working?" Joya repeated.

"I told you *we* were under construction," Chet broke in. "Derek is crew boss or something like that. If you convince your granny to fix Joya's Quilts he'd be the man to see. Him or the contractor, Preston Shore."

Joya would never have guessed the guy she'd met yesterday, who was now staring at the departing SUV, worked with his hands.

There was an awkward silence, finally broken by Chet. "Joya, Harley and I are thinking of going to Quills and getting coffee. Would you like a cup?"

Quills was the old diner on the corner. It had recently been turned into a combination stationery and bookstore. There was a little café in the back.

"Yes, please. Let me get you money."

"Our treat. How do you take it?"

Joya told Chet that she liked it light and sweet. She hurried back into the store to find LaTisha and Deborah's numbers. While she called LaTisha she rehearsed her sales pitch. Granny J needed to take full advantage of those loans. It would increase her property value if she made the place look good. But Granny J was from the old school, and believed that if you couldn't pay for something with your own cash you didn't need it.

Neither woman picked up, so Joya left messages.

She was on her own, not that there was a large crowd queuing up to be waited on.

Her first customer, a freckle-faced tourist in a straw hat with flowers and two toddlers clinging to the sides of her skirt, finally sauntered in around quarter to ten. The little boy, his mop of red curly hair sticking straight up, was sucking his thumb. The little girl grabbing onto the other side of her mother's skirt lapped at an orange Popsicle. Joya shuddered. She was an accident waiting to happen.

"Can I help you?" Joya asked, trying to smile pleasantly at the woman.

"Just browsing." The woman made a slow circle of the outer room, stopping to poke at the occasional quilt or pillow.

It would be easier on her anxiety level just to let them roam around. Curiosity, and the desire to take her mind off the potential accident, caused Joya to pick up the small notebook where Granny J recorded the daily sales. She flipped through several pages and found nothing. At least nothing recorded for almost a week. Could Granny J be getting senile or simply losing it? She'd always been meticulous about writing down even the smallest sale, whether it was quilting thread or the materials she sometimes sold for quilt-making.

Harley returned with her coffee just then, and Joya

put aside the notebook to look at later. Chet returned to the flower shop; having done his duty he wanted no part of her.

They'd butted heads a time or two, once when Joya had parked in front of their store. She'd only meant to run in to Joya's for a minute or so, but then she'd ended up helping Granny J with something or another. Chet had come out of his shop and loudly pointed out that this was a pedestrian-friendly street, yet it was ironic that he and his partner had done exactly the same thing this morning. It was always one thing or another. What was good for the goose was not good for the gander.

The mother and her two kids left, promising to return after a trip to the ATM. A few locals came in, browsed and departed. More tourists trickled in, but it was already late morning and so far not one sale.

Close to eleven o'clock, LaTisha skated in, sputtering apologies.

"Where's Granny J?" she asked, looking around the room as if she expected the old lady to materialize from a corner. Realizing that it was Joya she had to deal with, she smiled sheepishly. "Sorry, I had a flat tire. Ed at the service station couldn't get to it until now."

Joya glanced at her watch pointedly, "And you couldn't call? I left a message on your answering machine when you didn't show up when you were supposed to."

"Granny J doesn't have a problem with me being late," LaTisha said rudely.

"But I do, especially when I don't know what's going on. By the way, Granny J's not going to be in for a while. She's in the hospital. When she's released she'll need time at home to recuperate."

"But she was fine the last time I saw her."

Not, How is she? What can I do to help? Nothing.

"I'll need your help rearranging a few items," Joya said, changing the topic. She picked up some quilts from the bed and draped them on a divan that, wonder of wonders, held nothing.

"I'll help you as soon as I get back from getting coffee."

"I need help now. Where's Deborah? Has she been in touch with you?"

"I don't keep track of her comings and goings," LaTisha answered sulkily. She accepted the quilts Joya handed her and stomped off.

Joya was suddenly conscious of the man hovering at the front entrance. His energy was electric. It reached out and zapped her. Derek Morse stood at the doorway taking in the scene, aviator glasses still shading his eyes.

"Was there something you wanted?" Joya asked.

LaTisha did an amazing turn about when she spotted Derek. With a smile a mile wide, and rolling her hips she headed his way.

"Can I help you find something?"

Derek smiled vaguely at LaTisha as he entered the store. "Do you have a minute to talk?" He asked Joya, dipping his head at the saleswoman who looked as if she might hand him her panties any minute. "Privately."

Joya led him into the back room where the quilt guild met. She closed the door so LaTisha would not overhear them.

"Have a seat," she said, waving Derek toward one of the straight-back chairs that suddenly seemed ridiculously small. "What is it you want to talk to me about?"

Derek removed his sunglasses and set them down on the table. He sat, legs apart, blue jeans molding themselves over a bulge that Joya had no business gaping at. She suddenly wished for air-conditioning, something a heck of a lot cooler than the ocean breeze that floated through the open windows.

"I'd like you to speak with your grandmother," Derek said.

"About what?"

"Renovating the store. My crew's working on the florist's shop and the wine and cheese place to the right. This is the center store. If everyone surrounding her has a restored facade and updated interiors, Joya's is really going to look dated and worn."

While Joya didn't care for how he put it, he made a good point.

"My grandmother's a very stubborn woman," she said. "Part of the problem is she doesn't like owing anyone for anything."

"My great-grandmother is much the same. These ladies come from a different time. They didn't grow up with credit cards or equity lines they could dip into. I'm saying this because I don't want to see her lose out, especially when the bank is practically giving money away. Improving the store will increase the property value, and a refurbished exterior and interior will bring in a spending crowd."

Regardless of whether he was sincere, or simply out to feather his own nest, Derek made sense. And he didn't sound like any construction worker she knew. Not that Joya knew many. He'd presented his case in a well-thought-out and articulate manner. What he said was worth considering.

"I'll talk to Granny J after she gets out of the hospital," Joya agreed. "And we'll get back to you."

Derek rose, towering above her. He smelled clean, like soap, surprising because ripping out drywall, hauling debris and pounding nails usually made you sweat.

The phone rang, and Joya was glad to escape to get it. Something about being this close to Derek made her feel flushed and scatterbrained. She felt as if she'd been running a mile and couldn't catch her breath.

He waved at her and said over his shoulder, "Let me know what you and your granny decide."

Joya picked up the receiver of the old-fashioned phone.

"Hello."

"You left a message."

"Who is this?"

"Deborah."

The other saleswoman.

"Shouldn't you be here?" Joya asked.

"I don't feel well."

"And you're calling at this hour?"

There was a pause on the other end, then, "I'll be in tomorrow, if I feel better. It's payday and you owe me for the two weeks before."

Joya hung up, wondering how long these two had been getting away with murder. She couldn't imagine why Granny J would keep two losers like these on her payroll.

And then she remembered the woman's words. Granny J owed her for the two weeks before.

Perhaps it was time to take a closer look at her grandmother's books.

Chapter 3

"Too bad all of our jobs aren't like the one on Flamingo Row," Preston Shore, Derek's boss, said, clinking his bottle of beer against Derek's.

Derek took a slug of his own drink then said, "It's nice to be doing something different, preserving rather than destroying."

"I was talking about the fringe benefits. That Joya Hamill sure is eye candy. Just looking at her makes me horny."

Derek grunted something unintelligible and stuck his fingers in the bowl of peanuts on the bar. He tossed a handful in his mouth and chewed slowly and thoughtfully. Joya was attractive all right but definitely full of herself. The way she'd looked down her nose at him when he'd spoken to her in the store earlier. And he hadn't imagined it, either. He knew that look. He'd once had a woman just like her at home.

It was always, "gimme, gimme, gimme." That kind of demanding, self-focused woman could drain the life out of you. And he'd given until he'd had nothing more to give and then she'd walked away. Women!

"Okay, she's hot but obviously high-maintenance," Derek responded when Preston nudged him with his elbow. "She's also not at all what I'm looking for."

"What *are* you looking for?" Preston asked.

"I'll know her when I meet her."

Friendship aside, Preston had agreed to take Derek on as a worker, warning him up front that he'd better hold his own. Preston's big concern was that a trained engineer would not want to get down and dirty with the boys.

Derek had been forced to prove himself over and over. He now had the nicks, cuts, aches and pains that went with the construction business to show for it.

But he was happy. After years of corporate downsizing and sophisticated backstabbing, he was free of meetings and kowtowing to anyone. Now he showed up when he was supposed to, put in a full day's work and went home tired but content.

After the last restructuring at the aircraft-manufacturing company where he'd been a manager, he'd decided the stress just wasn't worth it. He'd left, taking his bonus and stock options with him. Derek's sights were now on owning his own construction business, and he'd decided he'd do what he needed to do to learn the job from the bottom up.

Preston was still waiting, regarding him carefully, an eyebrow hiked. "And Joya Hamill doesn't fit the bill of what you're looking for?"

Derek shook his head. He really didn't want to talk about women. He was over talking about women. But Preston was expecting an answer.

"Look, I don't want anything too hot or heavy right now. My energies need to be focused on learning all you can teach me about running a profitable construction firm."

Preston's index finger stabbed the air. "Gotcha! But you still gotta make time for fun. If I wasn't already involved, I'd be hooking up with Joya Hamill, that's for sure."

Derek couldn't help smiling. "Guess I've never been interested in trouble."

"Something about trouble can be appealing. Any of those babes worth a second glance?"

Derek surveyed the packed Haul Out where an after-work crowd was winding down. The patrons were primarily a blue- and pink-collar group, the men still in uniforms, name tags on their chest. Some played pool or darts off to the side while women with pumped-up boobs and gold ankle bracelets sat on high banquettes yakking up a storm and checking out would-be prospects.

"No babes," Derek said firmly. "Not until I get my own business up and running."

"Whatever."

They returned to their beers, and Derek indulged in a brief fantasy about a woman at the end of the bar with legs that wouldn't stop. Unfortunately the Hamill woman kept popping into his head, screwing up his sexy little daydreams.

He stared out onto the dance floor where a brunette who hadn't seen thirty in years and a coffee-skinned woman poured into tight capris jiggled everything they had in a desperate booty call. Except, no one was answering.

"It would be to everyone's benefit if you could convince the granddaughter to spruce up that quilt shop," Preston said, breaking into his thoughts. "I can't think of anything worse than having Joya's the only place on the Row not renovated. The place has such potential and the bank's practically giving money away with those interest-free loans plus a delayed period to pay back. It would be more money in our pockets, and I'd have the prestige of saying my firm had the monopoly of fixing up all the buildings on the Row."

Derek took a long pull on his beer. "True, and I've already put it out there. I mentioned that the centennial celebrations are bound to draw strangers to Flamingo Beach. Joya's not stupid; she has to know it's going to attract customers with spending power."

"And she said?"

"That she'd talk to her grandmother when she gets out of the hospital. You've got a bunch of jobs lined up so this one shouldn't make that big a difference."

Preston shrugged. "Call it pride or just the desire to have my stamp on the entire Row. If Granny J waits until the last minute to make up her mind we might be booked."

"Good point."

In some ways Derek hoped the old lady did just that. He didn't relish spending one more minute than he had to around the Hamill woman. The way she'd looked at him with those huge gray eyes had made him feel like yesterday's leftovers.

Preston shoved a handful of peanuts in his mouth and chased them down with beer. "Aren't your great-grandmother and the old lady friends? Can't you ask Belle for help?"

"I suppose so," Derek answered halfheartedly. He set down the empty beer bottle and reached for his wallet. "I gotta go. Gotta start work on my second job."

"This is on me," Preston said, stopping Derek before he could slap down a twenty. "It's your tab the next time around. Do you ever give yourself a break?"

"Not until Nana's house is finished. It might not look like much now, but by the time I'm done with it..." Derek placed curled fingers to his lips and kissed them. "See you tomorrow, Preston."

"I'll be there the usual time. Six."

Derek had his hands wrapped around the doorknob when Nana Belle's throaty voice reached him.

"Derek?" she called. "Is that you, boy?"

"Yes, ma'am."

It never ceased to amaze him that his wheelchair-bound great-grandmother, with her failing eyesight and poor hearing, knew almost to the second when he came home.

He opened the front door, left his muddy construction boots at the entrance and picked his way around drywall, heading toward the back of the house where Nana Belle lived.

The old lady spent most of her days seated in an overstuffed chair looking out at the water and smoking. Derek abhorred the habit, but figured that given Nana was almost one hundred years old and it hadn't killed her, who was he to say anything?

Nana Belle occupied the only room with an unobstructed view of the water. All of the other rooms had the boardwalk in between. Given the kind of life Nana had had, she deserved that one perk. Now she spent most of her day people-watching.

"How was your day, Nana Belle?" Derek asked dutifully kissing the old lady's weathered cheek. "Did you give Mari hell?"

Nana Belle wrinkled her nose and stuck out her lip. "I don't give anyone hell. Life's too damn short for that." She sniffed loudly. "You smell of beer. Shame on you. My Gideon never touched the stuff."

Gideon was Nana's third husband. She'd outlived five so far. Now with failing eyesight and bad hearing, Nana's olfactory senses had heightened. Derek thought she was amazing for a woman who'd seen almost an entire century go by.

Nana's aide, a long-suffering widow called Mari, took care of her. The two women fought constantly, usually because Nana was not eating and preferred to smoke. Nana Belle often told Mari to take a hike, and not in such pleasant terms.

The constant bickering made the old lady feel alive and important. She actually liked her aide, it was being dependent she hated, and it killed her not to be mobile and that she needed help to be bathed and dressed.

"How are the party plans coming?" Derek called to Mari, who was in another room.

When he'd left at the crack of dawn, the two women had been arguing over who would be on Nana's invitation list.

"I don't want no party," Nana said, spitting out her bridgework that she claimed was more painful than helpful. Her hollow jaws worked as if she was chewing on catfish.

"Done deal, Nana. You're getting a party whether you want one or not."

The old lady snorted. Deep down, his great-grandmother was very excited about her birthday party and was an active participant in selecting who was to be on the invitation list. It was her day and as far as Derek was concerned, she could invite the entire community. How many people could say they'd lived to see as many changes as she had? How many oldest living residents of Flamingo Beach were there?

It was going to be a huge event, and Derek thought about reserving the ballroom of the new Flamingo Beach Resort and Spa, since even Mayor Solomon Rabinowitz planned on attending. Tre Monroe, Warp's premiere radio personality was pre-recording an interview with Nana which he planned on airing on her birthday. That was another reason Derek needed to get these renovations done.

Word had gotten out about how big this event was. Now everyone and his dog were trying to wangle an invitation. Since the party was the same week as the centennial celebrations, T-shirts with the original map of Flamingo Beach with an X where Nana's house was located were already being sold. Nana Belle's party would go down in history and the house needed to look good.

Derek was pulling out all the stops and funding the party with money from his stock options. He didn't give a rat's butt about the tax implications. Nana Belle had given birth to twelve children, the results of three of her five marriages. She had fifty grandchildren, thirty-eight of whom were still alive, and twelve great-grandchildren. But Derek was the only one who'd volunteered to pay for the party. Without Nana he would not be where he was today.

So, he was determined that everything would be perfect, from the reserved parking space at the brand-new resort, should he decide to hold the event there, to the flowers provided by All About Flowers. The way Derek had it figured, the guest list would top out at one thousand people. But Nana had earned that kind of tribute.

Had it not been for her he would not have seen a college door. Somehow his great-grandmother had found the money and sent it to his parents. Derek suspected she'd mortgaged the very house he was working on.

It was Belle he had to thank for helping him get that master's degree in engineering. She'd ensured him a certain lifestyle and social status far different from his very humble upbringings. His parents had been forced to move in with relatives. He, on the other hand, had the means to live on his own. He lived with his great-grandmother because he wanted to.

"Mari, where are you?" Nana Belle called.

"Fixing you something. Be right in."

"I don't want nothing."

Derek tuned out the bickering that predictably would follow and thought about where he was today. He'd willingly chucked all the material things to pursue this current goal. He'd rented his fancy apartment in Chicago and traded in the luxury car for a pickup truck. He'd turned his back on the corporate world and the superficial friends that came with it to do something he much preferred—work with his hands. Now he didn't have to plow through a management minefield and kiss the asses of people he did not respect.

Enough of the meanderings, his second job called. Derek was not at all unrealistic. At some point Nana might have to move into an assisted-living facility and he would need a place of his own, especially if he decided to stay on in Flamingo Beach. A house this size, with all of its rambling additions, was expensive and exhausting to maintain, and definitely too big for one person.

"When was the last time you ate?" he asked his grandmother.

Nana lit a cigarette and blew a smoke ring in his direction. "You know Mari. She's always forcing food down my throat."

"And you keep saying you don't want anything. You just prefer to pull on those cancer sticks," Mari shouted from wherever she was.

No one, absolutely no one could force Nana Belle to do anything she didn't want to do. Derek smothered a smile and tried to avoid the cloud of smoke hovering over Nana's braided head. He made a U-turn and headed for the kitchen to find Mari and suggest she bring Belle a glass of the nutritional supplement she hated.

He continued into the dining area, removed his shirt and began to put up drywall. He thought that if he could make the house a showpiece in time for the centennial celebrations then Nana should be able to sell it and realize a good profit. He also thought about having her party at the house. Derek anticipated another huge fight with regard to selling her house, but the old lady could use the money for whatever she desired. She did not need to be leaving her house or hard-earned money to ungrateful relatives.

But try telling Belle that. It would take some doing, but Derek was determined to make his grandmother see things his way.

Over at Flamingo Beach General, Granny J was kicking up a considerable fuss.

"What do you mean you're not going to discharge me, young man?" she screamed at the doctor.

A patient Dr. Benjamin reached out a comforting hand to stroke Granny J's arm. "I'm not entirely satisfied with the results of your EKG. I'd like to run another test just to be sure."

"I want out. Now! There's nothing wrong with my heart."

Dr. Benjamin, used to dealing with recalcitrant elderly people, consulted his chart. Joya stepped in, taking Granny J's plump hand that was slapping the bed sheets in frustration as if it were Benjamin's cheek. Joya squeezed her grandmother's hand and spoke soothingly.

"It's only one more day. One day with your feet up isn't going to kill you."

"But one more meal in this place will," Granny J, who loved her food, mumbled. With age, her appetite hadn't slowed down one bit.

"May I speak to you privately?" Dr. Benjamin asked Joya, inclining his head to indicate that he wanted to talk outside of the room and not in her grandmother's hearing.

Granny J tugged her hand from Joya's hold and folded both arms across her chest.

"Whatever you have to say can be said in front of me. I'm not dead yet."

To Dr. Benjamin's credit he didn't lift so much as an eyebrow. "I don't think you'll be dying anytime soon, Mrs. Hamill, at least not from the sounds of you."

Joya stifled a grin. She liked the handsome doctor's way of handling the difficult old lady. He wasn't talking down to her. Dr. Benjamin was solidly built and had probably played football during college. He had a thick neck and broad shoulders.

It was his smile Joya liked. That smile could melt an icicle. The doctor wore his glasses on a chain around his neck, and he occasionally put them on to squint at the chart. Joya noticed there was no ring on his left hand or a tan line that said at one time there might have been.

She remembered the nurse yesterday saying there

was a girlfriend, and she supposed that would be the case. All the good ones were already taken. She'd lost a good one because of her own stupidity. Now Chere Adams would benefit from Joya's lack of patience and foresight.

Dr. Benjamin was waiting outside. She couldn't keep him.

"I'll be right back, Grandma," Joya said.

Granny J's plump hand covered her heart. "Lordie child, I must be dying. You never ever call me Grandma."

It was Joya's cue to leave before Granny J really got rolling. She made a hasty escape, her high heels tapping loudly on the white-tiled floor.

Outside she asked, "What did you want to talk to me about, Dr. Benjamin? Is Granny J's condition something I should be worried about?"

In the room she'd put on a good face, but now that she was no longer under Granny J's scrutiny, panic began to overtake her. Joya looked carefully at the doctor, hoping to get a hint of what he was really thinking.

"There may be some blocked arteries, all the evidence is there. I've ordered another EKG just to be sure."

"What!" The walls in the hallway wavered around her.

Dr. Benjamin, incredibly in tune, squeezed Joya's shoulder. "Take deep breaths. For a woman your grandmother's age she's in good shape. If the second EKG confirms what I believe, it should be a relatively simple procedure. She'll be up, around and as good as new in no time."

"Must be those damn pork rinds," Joya muttered, resorting to humor because tears were clouding her vision. It was easy for the doctor to say "simple procedure," it wasn't his grandmother.

"We'll wait until the results are back and we'll talk again and come up with a plan."

Translation: Granny J could easily be in the hospital for another few days. Gran would hate that.

Joya nodded and Dr. Benjamin squeezed her shoulder again. He was becoming a little too touchy, especially since he allegedly had a girlfriend. Joya wondered what was up with that.

"It might not have a thing to do with pork rinds," he said gently, smiling at her.

Since visiting hours were almost over, she ducked back into the room to see if Granny J needed anything.

"I told you to bring my quilting," the elderly woman grumbled. "I promised Elda I'd have that quilt done for her in a couple of weeks. Did that man ask you on a date?"

"What man?"

Joya knew exactly whom Granny J meant but decided to play with her.

"Dr. Ben. You've always wanted to marry a doctor."

"No, he did not and I never said I wanted to marry a doctor."

True, she'd hoped for security and had wanted to marry someone established. He didn't necessarily have to be a pretty boy. Granny J had warned Joya there was a lot more to marriage than a physical attraction. She'd been right. Quen was bright and one helluva lover, but he'd been underemployed. She'd seen his potential but had grown sick and tired of waiting for him to see it. Who would have thought he'd have moved from his interest in personal training to become a nutritionist? Now she had no one but herself to blame for losing a good man.

"Dr Ben has a girlfriend," Joya reminded her grandmother, not wanting to think about Quen. "When I come by tomorrow, you and I have something to talk about."

"Girlfriends come and girlfriends go. This isn't a wife we're talking about." Granny's forehead wrinkled. "What do you and I need to talk about?"

As Joya debated how to answer the question, images of a body that looked as if it might be carved from granite flashed before her eyes. Those faded, tattered jeans were molded over some pretty intimate places. And who could forget those hard biceps and that chiseled face with eyes that burned into you?

Derek Morse was the type of guy you didn't easily forget. Much as Joya wanted to dismiss the erotic vision of him that had surfaced, it kept coming back to her. A construction worker was not part of her plans.

An hour later, Joya sat at the bar of the Pink Flamingo waiting for her friend Emilie Woodward to show up. Mojito in hand, she stared up at the ceiling of the thatched tiki bar. Pink flamingos of various sizes fluttered from above. They were both cute and tacky and at the very least made for a good conversational topic.

Emilie was the Director of Leisure Sales for the Flamingo Beach Resort and Spa. She too lived in one of the condominiums at 411 Flamingo Place.

Where the heck was Emilie? Joya remembered she was habitually late and always blamed it on her job. Clients were running behind or simply didn't show up. Deals seemed to get screwed up at the last minute.

Emilie was relatively new to town and had been glad to meet Joya, who was around the same age. Joya liked that Emilie had no preconceived notions about her. Her friends in Flamingo Beach were pitifully few. Most had sided with Quen when the marriage had ended because they felt he'd got the crappy end of the deal. He was still paying her alimony.

While Joya sipped on her mojito she thought about how she and Emilie had met. Both of them had been huffing and puffing on a treadmill when they'd struck up a conversation. They'd found out they were both single and living in the same building. Hooking up seemed the obvious thing to do.

Conversation came easily. Who better to commiserate with about the poor pickings on the beach than another single woman? Joya had given up on finding the kind of man she was looking for in Flamingo Beach. It was only a matter of time before she'd have to return to Los Angeles and her flight attendant's job. Her leave of absence couldn't go on forever.

"Sorry I'm late," Emilie said, rushing in, wearing a dress with a plunging neckline and wide skirt. Green ferns were splashed across the beige material and matched her open-toed mules.

Several men swiveled on their stools to see who'd arrived. Emily's long red hair was pulled off her face and held back by beige combs. Physically, she and Joya were complete opposites. Whereas Emilie was tall, Joya was petite. Emilie was also so light-skinned that she was often mistaken for white. She had enormous boobs, swimmer's shoulders and the kind of face few people forgot.

She could have been a cover model for a men's magazine; she knew exactly the effect she had on men and made it work for her. She'd been living with a lawyer in South Jersey, hoping to marry him. But he'd left for work one day then forgotten to come home. Emilie later learned he'd moved in with one of his paralegals.

Skirt rustling, Emilie swung herself onto the vacant stool Joya had been saving. Joya couldn't help feeling underdressed and like Plain Jane next to her. Joya had barely made it back to the condo to take a quick shower and toss on a denim mini-skirt and spaghetti-strap shirt. Thank goodness she'd worn her signature high heels or she would have been a total frump.

"A cosmopolitan, please" Emilie said, smiling at the bartender before turning her attention back to Joya. "What's new with you, hon? How's your grandmother?"

Earlier, Joya had told Emilie about Granny J being hospitalized. Now she told her what Dr. Benjamin had said.

"Let's hope it's nothing serious. Doc is very good at what he does and I quite like him. He recommended me to friends. They've since bought time shares."

"I heard he had a girlfriend," Joya ventured.

Emilie looked at Joya through shuttered green

eyes. “It’s a long-distance thing I hear. I don’t think the doctor wants a woman underfoot 24/7.”

“What’s with Derek Morse?” Joya asked before she could stop herself.

“Not sure I know him.”

“He’s a construction worker. Doesn’t everyone know everyone in this town?”

“Not me. I’m new, but if he’s hot I’d like to meet him.”

“He’s hot in an obvious way.”

“What’s that supposed to mean?”

Most women would probably think Derek rocked.

“Maybe I need to be introduced to this Derek Morse,” Emilie said loudly.

A deep male voice came from behind them, making both women turn.

“Anything you ladies want to know about Derek Morse you can always ask me.”

A hulk of a man wreathed in gold chains was almost on top of them. Not waiting for an invitation to enter the conversation—he just spoke up.

Joya was mortified at having been caught talking about Derek. She quickly recovered and smiled animatedly at the stranger.

“I’m thinking about having Derek Morse do some work for me. What do you know about him?” she asked.

"In that case you'll be wanting to speak with Preston Shore. He's the contractor Derek works for and my old partner. I sold my part of the firm to him. I'm Vince by the way."

He stuck out a large paw and the women shook it.

"I think I'll join you," Vince said sliding onto the vacant seat next to Emilie. "You look thirsty, ladies, let me buy you a drink."

"This one is about all I can handle," Joya said after thanking him.

"I'll have another." Emilie pointed to her half-empty glass. Joya wondered why she was being so accommodating. She probably saw client potential in Vince.

Vince signaled to the bartender to bring a refresher. "Still interested in hearing about Derek?" he asked.

Just the sound of the construction worker's name created a warming effect. It must be the drink.

"Of course I am," Emilie said, leaning in close to Vince and batting her eyelashes.

"Well, he's only been back in town a couple of months. We think he lost his job in Chicago. He moved in with his great-grandmother Belle Carter."

"His great-grandmother?" Emilie scrunched up her nose. "What grown man lives with his great-grandmother?"

Vince sucked on his lower lip. "Derek's somewhere around thirty-five. He and Belle have always been close. She owns an old run-down house set back a bit from the boardwalk. There's plenty of room so that they don't interfere with each other."

Joya listened carefully as Vince spoke until two businessmen strolled into the bar wearing expensive suits and power ties. She found her attention wandering.

"Derek's one of these guys who doesn't stay with a job for any length of time," Vince added.

Joya's attention shifted to the businessmen who'd found a seat. She'd heard enough to confirm that Derek Morse was an irresponsible drifter.

Not that that came as a big surprise.

Chapter 4

The next morning Joya made a point of getting to the store early. After rummaging around, she found an old coffeepot and made coffee. Then, mug in hand, she went searching for another book where Granny J might have recorded her payroll and sales.

What her grandmother really needed was a computer, although it was doubtful the old lady would use it. Modern technology would be something that scared her. And she was definitely set in her ways.

But no amount of searching yielded a new book and the old notebook had not been updated. Joya finally gave up, deciding she would have a discussion with her grandmother when she saw her later.

A banging came from the front door. Joya hurried off to unlock it. Harley Mancini stood on the front step.

"Coffee? I'm making a run to Quills."

"No thanks. I found a pot and made some. You're welcome to have a cup."

"Thanks, but I'm thinking of getting a latte. Can I get you a Danish? Croissant, toast?"

Joya tapped her flat stomach. "Thanks, but no thanks. I seldom have breakfast."

Harley reached over and playfully tweaked one of Joya's slender arms. "Hon, those bones could use some meat."

Joya swatted him with the other arm. "I've worked very hard to keep weight off, and I'm not about to undo years of discipline. Where's your partner?"

"Chet's minding the store." Saying his partner's name seemed to propel Harley into motion. He glanced at his watch. "The construction crew's going to be here in exactly ten minutes. I'd better go get breakfast."

Joya waved him off and shut the door behind her. Construction crew meant Derek Morse. She wasn't sure she was up to seeing him again. But, her feelings about him aside, she now had two things to discuss with Granny J: taking advantage of those interest-free loans and figuring out whether the store was producing a profit.

She finished her coffee and decided that before the shop officially opened, she'd try to do something about the clutter. She was sure Granny J had quilts that she didn't even know existed stuffed in some places. Maybe she could have a sale and unload some of the merchandise that had been sitting. The problem was that she had no idea what had been here for some time and what was new. She needed the help of the saleswomen. Either that or she'd be forced to call Granny J. And that was something she was reluctant to do. Her grandmother needed her rest.

Half an hour past opening she still had no help. Neither Deborah nor LaTisha had shown up. By then, Joya had cleared off one table and scribbled a sign on a piece of white cardboard that said, Porch Sale. Cash Only! She'd found at least two dozen quilts shoved haphazardly in a garbage bag in the back room's closet. After running a practiced eye over them and determining that they would normally sell in the range of two hundred and fifty to four hundred dollars, she slashed that price in half.

She found a couple of toss cushions that looked as though they might have seen better days and added them to the pile of sales items. She also uncovered some smaller quilts that might serve as either wall hangings or baby blankets, and some quilted jackets.

It sounded as if someone was using a drill next door. The annoying buzzing put her on edge, but she was determined to ignore the noise.

She needed somehow to maneuver the table and its contents onto the porch. Where were those two lazy workers when she needed them?

Joya was using her hip and both hands to push the table in the direction of the outdoors when a deep male voice came from behind her.

"Would you like a hand with that?" Derek Morse asked.

"Yes, please." Joya's relief showed in her warm smile. She'd never thought she'd be happy to see Derek Morse, but he was certainly useful.

Effortlessly, Derek picked up the table, contents and all. He angled it through the doorway and onto the porch.

"Is this good?" he asked, setting it right behind the verandah railing.

"Just a little more to the right. That should do it."

Following her directions, Derek placed the table in the exact spot she'd pointed to.

"How's this?"

"Perfect."

He stood silently, his jeans hugging his high butt,

the knees threadbare, watching her spread a quilt over the table before folding and arranging the others. Without asking, Derek began arranging the sales items so that they were attractively laid out and could be seen.

"How about I tack the sale sign right up there?" he asked pointing to the back wall that badly needed a coat of paint.

"That would be great. Was there something you wanted?"

Derek took a hammer from the tool belt around his waist and pulled a nail from one of his pockets.

"Actually I came by to inquire as to how your grandmother is? Nana's been working herself up asking questions about your gran that neither me nor her companion can answer."

It made Joya feel good that her grandmother had friends who worried about her.

"Tell Belle Granny J's going to be fine. How did she find out my grandmother was in the hospital?"

"Not much escapes anyone in this town," Derek said over his shoulder.

Joya's eyes were fastened on Derek's wide shoulders and tapered waist. Where there were actual holes in the old jeans, you could see navy-blue underwear. Boxers actually. How many men today could pull off boxers and look sexy in them?

Derek pounded the nail into the wall and positioned the sign.

"What about right here?"

"Yes, that looks good. Thanks for all your help. Want a cup of coffee? I have a fresh pot brewing." She didn't know what made her extend the invitation, except that good manners dictated it. Much as she wasn't looking to start a friendship, Derek had come to her rescue at a time when she needed it.

Derek dusted off his hands. "I'll take a rain check. Gotta get back to work." He scanned the porch as if looking for someone. "Don't you have sales help?"

"Sore subject."

His words were a reminder that she needed to do something about those two. Granny J had put up with the two unreliable women, but that didn't mean she had to. They weren't exactly assets to the business. They weren't dependable and they sorely lacked customer-service skills. There was nothing like bad service to bring down a business.

Derek headed down the steps and then turned back. "Have you given any thought to what we discussed? You've got a pretty tight timeline to get back to us."

It took a second or two for Joya to figure out what he was getting at.

"I'd been hoping to talk to Gran when she gets out of the hospital, but maybe I'll do some preliminary investigation myself. What's the latest I can get back to you?"

"The end of the week. Shore Construction is booking quickly."

A gruff male voice called from next door. "Morse, where the hell are you? No one said you could take a coffee break."

"I'd better get back," Derek said quietly.

In the next half hour several passersby spotted the sales sign and wandered in. Joya sold two quilts and one of the pillows. At around ten-thirty Deborah and LaTisha were still not there.

Joya called both women but neither answered. She was at the end of her patience by then. The tourist with the redheaded children from yesterday came back, surprising Joya by buying one of the more expensive quilts and expressing interest in having one custom made. The woman was from Michigan. Joya took all of her relevant information, found out how long she was staying and promised to be in touch.

Right before lunch there was a brief lull in sales and Joya used that time to move the remaining sales items back indoors. She locked the store and decided to take the money to the bank. It would be a good opportunity to talk to Bill Brown, the loan officer. She might as well be properly informed if she was going to sell Granny J on the idea of applying for a loan.

There were long lines in front of the three tellers when Joya entered the lobby of the Flamingo Beach Credit Union. The credit union had been around forever, and despite another major bank opening up a branch, locals did most of their banking here where they were comfortable.

The three tellers were an institution, women close to sixty who knew everyone and needless to say everyone's business. Joya scanned the area in front of Bill Brown's office and was relieved to see that only one other person was waiting.

Joya signed the paper on the clipboard and took a seat in one of the overstuffed chairs. Ten minutes later the middle-aged man seated across from her was ushered into Bill's glassed-in office by his secretary, Marlene Miller, whom no one dared call anything other than Miss Miller. She was an aging spinster, way past retirement age.

"Mr. Brown will be with you shortly," Miss Miller said to Joya. "The senior Mrs. Hamill has sent you on her behalf, I assume?"

Joya nodded. To tell the old biddy it was none of her business would cause more trouble than it was worth. Since Joya's Quilts needed a loan it was best to suck it up. It would serve no purpose to alienate this woman.

"What you doing here, girl?" a high-pitched

female voice called from across the room, capturing the attention of everyone waiting for the tellers. "If I knew I'd run into you we could have scheduled lunch or something."

Today wasn't her day, Joya decided, watching her ex-husband's fiancée, exuberant as ever, come bouncing over. Chere had lost at least sixty pounds and although by no means skinny, appeared confident and sexy. Not that Joya disliked Chere, far from it. You couldn't help liking a woman who kept it real and called it like she saw it.

Joya met her halfway and the two women exchanged kisses. "Hi Chere, you look great as always. "How are the wedding plans coming?"

Chere rolled her eyes. "I never thought it required so much planning. You're coming, right? And you're bringing a date?

Joya assured her she was. She'd have to come up with a date somewhere.

Chere continued loudly, oblivious to who might overhear. "The Flamingo Beach Spa and Resort is really starting to tick me off. They're fighting me all the way over my entrée choices. I want to serve chicken, pork chops and steak. That's what Black people like, food that sticks to the ribs. I told that caterer it's my damn wedding and I can serve what I want. At least I did find a dress I like." Chere tapped her plump middle.

"It even makes my stomach look flat. And the photographer is all lined up and the deejay. As for centerpieces, well that's a whole other story."

"I'd think Chet and Harley of All About Flowers should be able to hook you up with the bouquets and table arrangements, no?" Joya tried not to burst into laughter as Chere did another eye roll.

"You'd think so, wouldn't you? But they're acting like it's a big deal because I want to keep things simple. I don't want no orchids or any of that stuff."

"What *do* you want?"

"Balloons, lots of them and candles, maybe just a couple of flowers here and there, nothing fancy. It's my celebration. I never thought this day would happen."

This time Joya did laugh out loud. It was good that they could chat like this, she thought. This must mean she was finally over Quen. Chere was obviously happy. She and Quen, though total opposites, were a good fit. Chere brought out the best in Quen. Joya should only be so lucky to find someone that completed her the way Quen did Chere.

"Miss Joya, Mr. Brown can see you now."

The two women kissed again. Joya, escorted by the over-vigilant Miss Miller, entered Bill Brown's office.

Bill, a man in his early forties, on the paunchy side and graying, presided behind a big oak desk with several golfing trophies on it. The wall behind him was glass and looked down on the busy main street. He stood when Joya entered.

"Just look at you. I remember when you were about this big. Knee-high to a grasshopper," he said, holding his hand palm down.

Bill was only a decade older than Joya, but his gray hair made him look much older.

She smiled graciously and shook the hand he held out. The preliminaries over with, Bill waved her to an overstuffed chair on the other side of the desk before sitting down again. "To what do I owe this pleasure?"

"I hear the bank is offering business owners interest-free loans to spruce up their properties. Is that true?"

"Yes, it's true. With the upcoming centennial only a few months away, we hoped to make Flamingo Beach a showplace. What surprises me is that your grandmother didn't take advantage of our offer. I assumed maybe financial difficulties and pride kept her from applying."

"Financial difficulties? What do you mean?"

A flutter of panic began in Joya's gut. Granny J had never said a word about having money problems. It wasn't until the two irresponsible saleswomen had claimed not to have been paid that Joya had sensed something might be wrong.

"From your expression I gather this is news to you," Bill Brown said rising and pouring them two cups of water from a pitcher. He handed Joya one.

She nodded, finally managing, "Just how bad is it?"

Brown stroked his smooth chin. "Well, let's see. Your grandmother came in about a year ago to get an equity line of credit. She was keeping up fine and then a couple of months ago she began falling behind."

"I see," Joya said, although she didn't see at all. "Exactly how much money does Granny owe?"

Bill turned his attention to the monitor on his desk, pecking on his keyboard. He made some rapid calculations and eventually named a figure.

It wasn't an astronomical amount. Joya had enough from today's sale to pay up the loan and still have a few dollars in reserve.

Joya fished in her purse, removed the envelope holding this morning's take from the sales, and carefully counted the bills out. She separated the money into two piles.

"I'm here to make the payments on that loan," she said, "I don't have Granny J's book with me. I'm also here to discuss getting one of those low-interest loans with you."

Bill pushed a button on the intercom.

"Yes, Mr. Brown," came Marlene Miller's querulous voice.

"Will you come in, please."

Miss Miller entered and stood reverently before Bill's desk.

"Will you please deposit this money in Mrs. Hamill's equity account," Bill said, "The other money goes to her checking. Bring me back both receipts." He scribbled what Joya assumed were both account numbers on a yellow pad, tore out the sheet, and handed it to Marlene.

"Certainly." Tossing a curious look Joya's way, Miss Miller turned and left them.

"So you wanted to talk about a loan?" Bill Brown said.

"Yes, I do. The stores around Granny's shop are all being renovated. I don't want Granny J to miss out. She's owned her property for almost as long as Flamingo Beach has been around. It would be a shame to let it go down."

"I agree."

For the next fifteen minutes, Bill told Joya about the loan options and the terms available. He told her she could fill out her application online and that she would receive approval in less than twenty-four hours.

"Will Gran's delinquent payments affect her getting this loan?" Joya asked. "You did say she was dutifully making the payments up until a couple of months ago?"

"Your granny has been a very good customer of

the credit union. Except for the equity line, she owns the building out right."

Marlene Miller was back, handing her tangible proof of the transactions. "That copy has your grandmother's balance," she quickly pointed out.

Joya thanked her and stood. Bill, always the gentleman, stood and followed her to the door. He handed Joya a couple of folders.

"Read this information and discuss it with Mrs. Hamill, then get back to us. You have my personal guarantee you will have your loan."

After shaking Bill Brown's hand and thanking him, Joya left.

As Joya came up the walkway she spotted Deborah and LaTisha, both looking somewhat put out. They sat on the porch step, gazing out onto the street.

"We've been waiting for hours," LaTisha pouted.

A slight exaggeration. Joya had only been gone for maybe an hour.

"You're late for work," Joya said, not cutting them any slack. "If you'd been here on time I wouldn't have had to lock up."

"It's payday. We need our money," both said in unison.

Deborah stood, stretching. "You owe us for two weeks plus this week."

Joya had been prepared for something like this. She had the feeling these two had been getting away with murder for quite sometime.

"You haven't worked this week," she quickly pointed out.

"I did," LaTisha hastened to say.

"Half a day and barely," Joya countered. "Let's go inside."

The business could remain closed for another fifteen minutes while she did what she needed to do. She was going to make an executive decision and not consult Granny J.

Joya was betting both women were minimum-wage employees. She did some rapid calculations. What was left of the proceeds of this morning's sale would barely cover two weeks' salary for both ladies, and if she were to give them another two days' pay as a token, it would pretty much clean the business account out.

But the afternoon was young and she was counting on selling the remainder of the sale items plus a few new ones. She unlocked the front door and allowed both women to precede her in. Then she locked the door behind her.

"Let's go into the back room," Joya said.

The two saleswomen, anticipating money, followed eagerly.

Joya quickly wrote out two checks and handed one to each individually.

Without even a thank-you, Deborah folded hers and placed it in her purse. LaTisha stuffed hers in the pocket of the low-rise Capri's she'd come supposedly to work in.

"We have to go to the bank. We'll be back shortly," LaTisha said.

Joya didn't say a word until they were out on the porch.

"No need to return," she said, following them out. "You're both fired."

"What!" This came from LaTisha. "You can't fire me."

"Your services are terminated. You're done."

Deborah, the darker of the two, tugged on a braid, her wine-colored eyes smoldering.

"You ain't my boss. The only person who can fire me is your grandmother."

"Okay then, pretend that I'm her. You're terminated. Fired. If you're not off the premises in exactly five minutes, I'm calling the police."

Chapter 5

"Bitch! You haven't heard the last of this!" LaTisha shouted, waving her fist in the air.

"Who you think you playing with?" Deborah called equally as loudly.

The shouting and threats had been going on for the last twenty minutes, ever since Joya had let the saleswomen go. The adjoining business owners were unusually quiet and hadn't made their presence known. They probably did not want to get involved.

But having that kind of scene out front was not helping business. She needed customers. Joya's Quilts needed the money.

Having had enough, Joya picked up the phone, determined to follow through with her threat of calling the police, but things had quieted down outside. Why? Curiosity brought her to the window. Derek Morse was speaking with the two ex-employees. She wondered what he was telling them. She debated going out there, then decided it would serve no useful purpose.

Whatever Derek said worked, because shortly thereafter Deborah and LaTisha left. Joya opened the door and stepped out onto the porch, bringing with her the remaining items for sale, plus several other pieces of merchandise.

Derek, most likely on a break, sat on a bench on the sidewalk shaded by a huge palm tree. He held a bottle of water in one hand and a sandwich in the other. This reminded Joya that she still hadn't eaten. She placed the merchandise on the table and stood, debating whether to say anything to him.

Chet Rabinowitz, who'd probably had his nose pressed against the window watching all the action, came out of his flower shop and ambled up the walkway.

"I was just about to call the police," he said. "What's going on?"

"I had to fire the two women and they're angry," Joya said.

"You fired the part-timer, too?"

Joya didn't know there was a part-timer and said so. "What part-timer?"

"Portia Cortez, she's a nice girl. She attends the community college and works on weekends or whenever the shop gets busy."

Joya made a mental note to call this Portia Cortez and see what her schedule was like. With the two women off the payroll, and scheduling sales help only in a pinch, maybe Joya's Quilts could start making some money.

"About time you had a sale and moved some of your old merchandise," Chet groused, mounting the steps and beginning to sort through the merchandise. "I need something for my guest room, but it has to be the right shade of green."

"If you find anything, let me know," Joya said magnanimously, "And I'll reduce it another twenty percent."

"That's an offer I'd be stupid to refuse." Chet unfolded a version of the Diamond Strip and shook out the quilt. He scrutinized it carefully. "This one has my name on it."

"Good choice," Joya said, tracing the outlines of the diamond-shaped pattern. "In African textile tradition the diamond symbolizes the cycles of life. Each point represents a crucial stage. Birth, life, death, rebirth, you know, all the passages of life."

Granny J had taught Joya everything she knew about the history of quilting. Chet's eyebrows were up to his hairline. He seemed surprised by her knowledge. It was time to bury the hatchet with him, Joya decided. Better to have him on her side than not. With a mouth like Chet's and a powerful father like Mayor Solomon Rabinowitz, he could make things mighty uncomfortable for Gran, even though he professed to like the old lady.

"I'm off to get my checkbook," Chet said, handing Joya back the quilt and starting down the steps. "Hey, you beautiful man," he called to Derek, "Didn't you say you needed a gift for your great-grandmother's birthday? Now might be the time to get it. Joya's is having a sale." To Joya he said in a loud whisper, "You will extend to him the same courtesy you did me? The additional twenty percent? He got rid of those two nasty bitches for you."

"Sure."

Derek Morse tossed the remainder of his half-eaten sandwich in a nearby trash can. Standing, he wiped his palms on the legs of his soiled and ripped jeans and reluctantly sauntered up the walkway, stopping to do one of those shoulder bumps men do with each other.

He and Chet were as different as night and day. Chet was average height and lean, with a pointy face that reminded Joya of a fox. Derek, on the other hand, was at least six foot two with wide shoulders, a narrow waist and long legs. He was the kind of man that ate up your breathing space and made you think of sex. Standing next to him made her nervous and made her forget what she was going to say.

Derek was now on the veranda and standing very close to her, and even though Joya was wearing her signature high heels he made her feel like a midget.

"What have we here?" Derek said, fingering a version of the Log Cabin pattern. Joya hoped his hands were clean. The quilt was yellowing with age anyway but she didn't need grease on it. She was being mean-spirited, she decided. The man had just gotten rid of two women making a scene out front of the establishment. She could be more gracious.

"Do you like it?"

His head listed to one side, thinking. "Actually, what I would like is a quilt to commemorate Nana Belle's life. Something she can choose to hang or use."

"You're looking for a custom quilt then. That will cost you a bit."

Derek stared intently at her through those hooded eyes of his and she felt her mouth go dry.

"I am prepared to pay whatever it might cost. It's not every day someone lives to be a hundred," he said tightly.

But did Derek know how much such a quilt might cost? It could easily run him a thousand, possibly more.

She managed to smile, hoping it did not come off as patronizing.

"We'll work something out. Thanks for getting rid of those two for me. It's not been a good day so far. Perhaps you might find something you like inside. I can work out a payment plan if you like. It's the least I can do."

"I don't need a plan." He didn't offer an explanation as to what he'd said to the women, just continued sorting through the sales merchandise, folding them neatly and returning them to their original spots.

"How about we discuss the custom quilt," he eventually said. "How long will that take and what will I need to do?"

He wasn't getting it. What he was asking for was going to be expensive.

"Are you thinking of something similar to a quilt popular in the mid-1800s titled the Black Family Album? There have been several knock-offs since. What happens is the quilter uses an appliqué technique to literally paste the person's family album onto the fabric. African tribes have done it and it was very popular in early-American tradition. It's one lasting way of recording family events."

"Exactly what I'm looking for," Derek said,

brightening. "I have to get back to work. Can I stop by afterward so we can discuss this album idea in greater detail?" He hesitated for a moment. "Better yet, allow me to buy you a latte at Quills after you close shop. That way I have your complete attention and you're not worrying about customers."

Now it was Joya's turn to hesitate. "After work I need to go to see my grandmother at the hospital. I plan on talking to her about getting the shop fixed up." She hesitated for a moment and then thought, what the hell, he wasn't an ax murderer. "If you'd like to stop by my place later, we can talk about the type of quilt you're looking for and I can tell you if Granny's agreed to move forward with the renovation."

"Okay, it's a deal. Give me your address."

Joya scribbled her address on the back of the store's business card and Derek pocketed it.

"Gotta get back to work," he said. "See you later."

Intrigued, though she was reluctant to admit it, Joya watched Derek swagger confidently down the steps.

Reality soon hit. She'd invited a man she didn't really know to her apartment. Was she losing her mind? At least Derek would be required to sign in at the reception desk, and his great-grandmother was a friend of her own grandmother. He wasn't entirely a stranger.

Meeting him in a public place would have made

more sense, but that would only create gossip. If they'd met at the Pink Flamingo, the Catch-All or even the Haul Out, then busybodies like the Flamingo Place resident gossip, Camille Lewis, would have them on a date. Joya didn't want anyone to get the wrong impression.

Two tourists slowed down and spotting the sale sign made their way up the walkway. Joya went back into the store, allowing them to browse in private. After about ten minutes the taller of the two stuck her head in the door, holding up one of the quilted pillows.

"Is this the best you can do?"

"Prices are as marked, but if you buy more than one item I might be able to do something."

Both women purchased two pillows. Their presence drew several others and Joya sold another quilt and a wall-hanging. By the time she closed the store at the end of the day she was feeling pretty proud of herself. It was too late to do any banking so Joya tucked the money in her pocket, got into her BMW, put the top down and drove to the hospital.

When she arrived, Granny J was fighting with the nurse's aide. Refusing to be intimidated, the young woman stood her ground.

"I want real food, not that hogwash you're

serving," Granny J said wagging a finger at the skinny child-woman.

"Everything on your tray is very nutritious, Mrs. Hamill."

"No, it's not."

"Gran, please settle down and stop being a bully," Joya said, intervening. She winked at the poor girl, who seemed unfazed by the treatment. "Leave the tray. I'll take over from here."

"I'll be back," the young woman said, vacating the room.

"How are you, Gran?"

"How do you expect me to be?"

"Pleasant and courteous, like you taught me to be."

Granny J glared at Joya. "How are things at the store?"

"I had a sale today. We did well."

"Sale? What sale? Joya's Quilts has never had to put merchandise on sale."

"And maybe that's the problem. You have too much inventory and not enough money coming in."

Granny J stuck her lower lip out. "Most of those quilts I accept on consignment. I hope you didn't sell anything too cheap."

"If I did," Joya said, not backing down, "They needed to be sold cheap. A lot of the items were yellowing or had visible flaws."

"Humph."

Without waiting to be invited, Joya sat on the chair next to Granny J's bed. "How are you feeling, Gran?"

"Awful!" The old woman said, folding her arms and making a face at the food in front of her.

"Then, in that case, I'd better get your nurse or even better, the attending doctor." Joya reached for the phone on the nightstand.

Granny J's fingernails dug into Joya's arms. "No, don't do that."

"But if you're not feeling well, Gran?"

"I feel perfectly fine. It's that doctor who says I'm not well. He says I need a procedure."

Although Dr. Benjamin had alluded to the fact that this might be a possibility, Joya felt her panic build. Granny being out of commission put a whole different spin on things. Joya had hoped she would be released in a day or two. But from the sounds of things that wasn't about to happen. Then there would be recuperation time. L.A. International would definitely not approve another extended leave of absence. They were already putting pressure on her to come back.

"Before I find your nurse, I'd like to ask for your permission to apply for a business-improvement loan." Joya held a hand up before Granny J could interrupt. "Hear me out, please." She went on to explain all the pros of getting a loan with a low interest rate, ending with, "We'd be pretty stupid not to take advantage of this money. Everyone around us is fixing up their places. Why should we be the only eyesore on the row?"

"Joya's Quilts is not an eyesore," Granny J huffed.

"The building needs renovating, Gran. We need to keep up."

"We do not. We manage fine. Besides, I hate owing anybody anything."

"We already owe the bank. Fixing up the place will only benefit us and help bring more revenue in. Tourists prefer to shop in nice surroundings."

"How did you find out about my equity line? Never mind. Okay, apply for the loan if you must."

"That's a good decision, Gran." Joya squeezed the old lady's hand and decided not to ask Granny J about why she'd failed to make her payments on time. She suspected she already knew. She also decided not to mention the firing of the two lazy employees. She didn't need her grandmother getting further upset, not with an operation and long recuperation period ahead.

"Now that we've gotten that squared away, I'm going to find your nurse," Joya said, rising. "She can call Dr. Benjamin and he can explain to me just what's going on. When I return there'd better not be one scrap on that plate."

Granny J stuck out her lower lip. The battle of wills was on.

Joya set off purposefully down the hallway, heading for the nurses' station. The medical team for the most part now differed from that of the night before, although Joya recognized one or two nurses.

"Can I help you?" a thickset nurse with a serious expression asked.

"I need to know what's going on with Mrs. Hamill. She tells me her doctor recommends surgery."

"And you are?"

"Her granddaughter. I'm her next of kin."

With one eyebrow slightly lifted, the nurse looked Joya over. Then, making up her mind, she said, "I'll see if I can get Dr. Ben to call in. He can explain the diagnosis to you."

"I'd appreciate that."

As Joya waited for the nurse to page the doctor, she prepared herself for the worst. Dr. Ben had told her last evening what he'd suspected and now the reality of the matter was about to hit home.

Deep in her gut she had the feeling she wouldn't be returning to Los Angeles anytime soon.

Chapter 6

By the time Joya's intercom buzzed she'd showered, changed and was close to wearing the polish off the lovely wooden floors. She'd just spent the last fifteen minutes pacing back and forth looking blankly at the to-die-for ocean view. What had possessed her to invite Derek Morse to come by? She had a lot on her mind with Granny J's upcoming surgery. Plus the man made her uncomfortable.

Joya had been fortunate enough to sublet one of Quen's apartments. That ex-husband of hers had turned into quite the entrepreneur.

"Yes?" she inquired after depressing a button on the wall.

"Ms. Hamill, a gentleman by the name of Derek Morse is here to see you."

"Send him up."

Joya did some rapid calculations in her head. If Derek took the stairs he'd be up in maybe three minutes. If he had to wait for the elevator it might take a little longer. Either way it gave her enough time to race into the bathroom and check to make sure she didn't have broccoli in her teeth or something like that. She gave a quick glance in the full-length mirror, reassuring herself she looked okay.

Joya had pulled her hair back into a ponytail and wrapped a green scrunchie around the rubber band she'd used to keep it back. There wasn't even a hint of a wisp escaping. Her white shorts were cuffed above the knee and didn't expose too much leg. The green-and-white striped T-shirt came down to cover her butt. Guaranteed she looked much younger than her thirty-three years, but what the hey.

The doorbell rang as she was debating whether she should change her flip-flops. Heels really didn't go with the outfit so now Derek would get to see how short she really was.

"Who is it?" she asked, before putting an eye to

the peephole. She already knew who it was, but one couldn't be too careful these days.

"Derek Morse."

"Just a minute,"

It took her longer than she anticipated to remove the security chain and open the double-bolted locks, she'd grown all thumbs.

Derek had changed his clothes, too, and managed a shower. He smelled of soap again. His jeans were spotless and had a sharp seam in the front indicating they'd been pressed. The crew-neck shirt he wore was the perfect shade of copper to complement the orange tones of his dark skin.

Joya tried her best not to stare at his large hand holding something that looked like a photo album; the nails were meticulously trimmed, not a hint of dirt under them. It was hard to believe construction was his profession.

She stood for a moment looking up at him, feeling completely dwarfed and more than a little overwhelmed. She needed to move, get away from him. Right now Derek was just too much man for her. She hadn't been this ruffled by anyone since Quen.

"Can I get you something? Coffee, a beer?"

"Water if you have it. Nice place."

"It's not mine. I rent." Joya headed toward the kitchen to get Derek his water.

"Nice view," Derek said, stalking toward the window wall that looked directly out onto Flamingo Beach. He set his photo album down on the coffee table. "It's especially great when you don't have something like a boardwalk creating an obstruction."

Joya returned to hand him a cold bottle of water. "I hope that brand's okay."

"It's fine with me. Water is water."

"Have a seat," Joya said, wanting to get as far from him as physically possible. He really did make her nervous, something she didn't understand.

Derek sat on the mint-green couch, legs splayed out in front of him.

"You mentioned you wanted to have a commemorative quilt made up for your great-grandmother's birthday," Joya prompted.

"Yes, Nana Belle is turning one hundred at almost the same time as this town is celebrating its hundredth birthday. I've planned a big birthday party and I've been wracking my brain trying to come up with a practical yet special gift. When I saw your quilts today they seemed like they would make the perfect gift."

"A custom quilt is the ideal gift for someone as special as your great-grandmother. She's something of an icon in this town." An idea was beginning to percolate in the back of Joya's mind. Being that the centennial was coming up, if Joya's Quilts could sell commemorative quilts she'd bet they'd rake in the money. The tourists would love it, and if she took orders in advance and got deposits the store could stay in the black. She made a mental note to discuss the idea with the quilting guild. It would mean lots of work for them as well.

"May I?" Joya asked, reaching for the family album that Derek had laid on her coffee table.

"Sure."

Eagerly she leafed through the scrapbook: pictures of Nana Belle as a young girl, her five marriages, the births of her children, their graduations, birthday parties, weddings and deaths. All the important passages of life were celebrated in the pages of that book. There were newspaper articles, menus from restaurants, wedding invitations, death announcements and photographs of Flamingo Beach at various stages of development. There were pictures of Nana Belle's home as it had started off as a two-room cabin then grown and grown. Here was the old lady's whole life encapsulated in one book. Joya'd bet anything Belle had some good stories to tell.

Heat settled in her cheeks as Joya sensed Derek

watching her. She closed the album and handed it back to him.

"Think of the quilt as scrapbooking, it would be a gradual progression of Nana Belle's life and something she will forever treasure," Joya said.

"She'd like that," Derek seemed contemplative. "We could scan images, articles etc. right onto the cloth."

"Exactly."

Joya ventured a look at Derek. His toffee-colored eyes held her gaze for a second too long. She was the first to look away. She couldn't deny the attraction, but Derek Morse wasn't what she was looking for. She wanted someone more ambitious; a man who was going to go places and take her with him. As Granny J was fond of saying, romance without finance is a nuisance. Joya had been there and done that. It wasn't a place she ever wanted to be again. It was no fun eating chicken backs and necks 24/7 just so you could pay the rent.

"How long will a quilt like this take to make?" Derek asked, breaking into her musings.

"If I can find someone dedicated to doing it, I'd say a month. What will take time is selecting what you'd like to have on the quilt and transferring the images onto the material. And..." Joya took a deep breath before continuing. "It's going to be expensive."

"How expensive?"

Derek was watching her intently. She was developing a shortage of breath that wasn't normal when you were sitting and not exerting yourself. Joya named a figure and waited.

Derek's long low whistle told her clearly what he thought.

She needed to make this work. Nana Belle and Granny J were friends and had been for a long time.

"How about we split the gift?" Joya suggested.

"Why?"

Derek had suddenly gone all steely-eyed on her. She hadn't meant to insult him.

She rose and crossed over to the window. While she wasn't sure she liked Derek Morse, that should have nothing to do with it. This was about the friendship between her grandmother and Belle.

"Your great-grandmother and my granny are friends," Joya said. "Since my gran would be giving yours a gift anyway, why not make it joint, memorable and something Nana Belle wants?"

Derek rose, too.

"I didn't come here looking for charity."

"I'm not offering you charity."

"I'd prefer to pay for the quilt on my own," he said more quietly.

"As you wish. I'll talk to one of the guild and get

back to you. You'll need to discuss color schemes and fabrics, that kind of thing. I've just thought of something else."

"What?"

This time Derek did come over to join her at the window.

"I'm thinking that when you send out your invitations to some people special to Belle you could include a block. Have the invitee write a message and sign it using indelible ink, and then have them get it back to us by a certain time."

"What's a block?"

"A square of fabric that you'd sew together to make your quilt."

Derek's long and meticulously clean fingers stroked his chin. "I like that idea. The quilt would be both a photo album and an autograph book."

"Exactly."

"On another note, did you have chance to talk to your gran about renovating the shop?" Derek asked, getting much too close. She could smell the soap on his skin.

Joya took a step back, putting space between them. Why would Derek care? What was in it for him other than making sure he had work?

"I did," Joya answered, "And she's finally agreed to take out a loan. When can we start construction?"

From Derek's startled expression she could tell she'd taken him by surprise.

"I'll need to speak with Preston Shore, the owner of my construction firm."

"Would you rather I talk to him directly? I'd like to make this happen sooner rather than later."

Derek shrugged. "As you wish. I'll have Preston call you tomorrow. And you'll get back to me tomorrow about that quilt and how soon it can be done?"

"I will."

Derek stuck his hand out and wrapped Joya's small hand in his. A bolt of electricity shot up her arm. Derek must have felt it too because he dropped her hand like a hot potato and quickly turned toward the door.

Joya's cell phone, clipped to the waistband of her shorts, rang, a welcome distraction. She glanced at the dial, frowned and hesitated.

"Aren't you going to get that?" Derek said pointedly.

"Hello… Yes, Chet? Our alarm went off?… The cops are there?…I'm on my way."

Joya depressed the button cutting Chet Rabinowitz off before he could say another word.

"I have to get to the quilt shop," she jabbered, picking up her car keys and purse from the kitchen counter where she'd left them. "That was Chet Rabinowitz. He's working late at the flower shop. Someone might have broken into the store."

"I'll drive you," Derek Morse said calmly, taking Joya by the elbow.

Joya didn't consider fighting him. This was one time she needed support, and having a solid presence like Derek while she dealt with the police and filled out paperwork would be welcome.

"I'd really appreciate that," Joya said, meaning it, as, accompanied by Derek, she raced for the door.

She didn't protest when Derek suggested they take his pickup truck. She simply slid into the front seat and they roared off, breaking every speed limit there was in Flamingo Beach.

Flamingo Row was humming with activity when they pulled up. The town's two police cars were parked outside the quilt shop where a small group of people were gathered, amongst them Harley Mancini and Chet Rabinowitz. An eager young reporter wearing a *Southern Tribune* polo shirt stood on the sidewalk accosting anyone he could.

Forgetting the man who had brought her here, Joya leapt from the vehicle and pushed her way through the people gathered. She ignored the hands tugging on her clothes and the questions being thrown at her from the crowd. Right now the only people she would talk to were the police.

Greg Santana, whom Joya had gone to high school

with, was in the middle of taking a statement from a shop-owner when Joya interrupted him.

"What's going on?" Joya asked, planting herself in front of Greg.

"Your burglar alarm went off. No one answered when the security company called to check on you. So here we are."

"They must have Gran's home phone number. She's in the hospital so there's no way they would reach her," Joya said out loud, resolving to call the security company and give them her cell number once this mess was sorted out.

"Find out anything?" Derek asked Greg. Joya had almost forgotten about him. And here he was asking the kinds of questions she should be asking.

Greg pointed his flashlight in the direction of a broken window. "See over there? Someone hurled a rock through the window and that in turn set off the alarm. Of course, by the time we got here there was no one in sight."

"Have you spoken to Chet?" Joya asked. "He called me with the news, mentioning he was working late at the flower shop. Maybe he saw something."

"We've spoken to both owners. Lionel and I have walked around the property and up and down the row several times. No one claims to have seen anything."

"That's strange." This came from Derek. "No one misses a thing in Flamingo Beach."

"Lionel and I aren't worried. We'll get a lead. Someone will talk. You must have keys to the shop, Joya. Let's go in and take a look around."

Joya rummaged through her purse and found the keys to the quilt shop. Greg, taking charge, cleared a path so that she and Derek could follow him.

As she mounted the steps and climbed onto the front porch, she remained hopeful that other than the broken window there'd been no further damage. Greg and Derek flanked her as she turned the knob on the front door. It was still locked and she exhaled a breath.

"No signs of forced entry," Greg said, shining his flashlight on the door's surface.

Joya inserted her key and after several tries the lock yielded. She was about to step inside when Derek moved her firmly out of the way.

"Let us go first. Coming?" he said to Greg.

Greg puffed himself up and Joya saw a power play coming. She stood aside and the two men preceded her in.

The showroom and working area looked just as they had when she had left, nothing visibly out of place. Joya wandered from room to room accompanied by the two men. She looked around to see if anything was missing. Not that she had a really good sense of the inventory, what she was looking for were empty spots where something might have been.

"I don't think whoever threw that rock actually broke in," she announced after several minutes of this. "Things are still in their place, plus the back door is locked and bolted."

"Someone might have wanted to get your attention. Have you or Granny J had an altercation with anyone recently?" Greg asked, his pad out, jotting notes.

Joya thought about the two employees she'd fired and the threats that they'd made. She told Greg about firing Deborah and LaTisha. He continued to scribble.

"Okay, no signs of forced entry, everything in order," he said, "We'll continue talking to the shop-keepers on the strip as well as anyone in the direct vicinity. What are you going to do about the window?"

Shoot. It was something she hadn't thought about. It was late, after nine, the locksmith would be closed.

"I'll take care of it," Derek said. "I have plywood in the bed of my truck. I can get that window boarded up in minutes."

"If you'd do that I'd be grateful. I'll pay you whatever it costs."

"That won't be necessary."

Derek sounded as if she'd offended him. Before she could explain or apologize, he was already heading for the front door.

"What's next?" she asked Greg.

"There's not much more to do here. We've determined the store hasn't been broken into so we'll put it down to vandalism. Lionel and I will have a conversation with the two young ladies. Get the window boarded up and go home and have a good night's rest. We'll be in touch." He shut his notebook.

The sounds of hammering came from outside. Derek was already busy putting up the plywood. Joya made sure the remaining windows were closed and latched. She checked the back door again, made sure it was secure and followed Greg out.

The few people left on the street were talking in loud voices. Bits of the conversation drifted over.

"This town has never had anything like this happen."

"Things are changing and not for the better."

"It's all the new people moving in and not the most desirable elements either."

Naysayers.

Lionel was seated in his police car, the red siren lights still going, waiting for Greg.

"Are you going to be okay? Do you need a ride home?" Greg asked,

"I'll be fine." Joya still felt a bit dazed and didn't know what to make of the whole thing. A rock hurled through the window of Joya's Quilts was big news and might even make the front page of tomorrow's *Tribune*.

"We'll gladly give you a ride," Lionel insisted, sticking his head out of the police vehicle.

Sweet as the offer was, if she arrived back at Flamingo Place in a police vehicle, the rumor mongers, specifically resident gossip Camille Lewis, would have it that she had been arrested.

"Derek drove me here. I'm sure he won't mind taking me home."

"What's with you and Derek?" Greg asked boldly. "You guys got something going on?"

Before Joya could respond to what she thought was a totally inappropriate question, Derek's voice came from behind her.

"Joya, come over and see if I've boarded up the window to your satisfaction. Then I'll take you home."

She wondered just how much Derek had heard of the conversation. His expression gave nothing away.

"Greg, Lionel," she said, "You'll call me when you find anything out?"

"Of course we will."

Lionel started up the police vehicle and the two men drove off.

Derek then surprised Joya by throwing an arm around her shoulder and giving it a little squeeze.

"You've had quite the night. You must be exhausted."

"I am," Joya admitted, surprised that she found

comfort in a little thing like having a man's arm around her shoulders. Not any man's arm—Derek's.

"So should I take you home or should I take you out for coffee with me?"

"Coffee would be nice," she shocked herself by saying.

"Then coffee it is, and how about a little key lime pie thrown in for good measure?"

Derek squeezed her shoulder again and she shivered. Why was she having a crazy reaction to this man?

Nothing could come of it. A construction worker was just not part of her plan.

Chapter 7

"You didn't grow up in Flamingo Beach?" Joya asked when she was settled comfortably into one of Mario's worn pleather booths.

"I was born here, but my parents moved up north when I was two."

Derek wondered whether Joya was genuinely interested in knowing or just making conversation. She was hard to read. She'd been chattering at him non-stop from the minute they'd walked into the diner, the only restaurant in town that stayed open after nine.

"How about you?" Derek asked.

"Born here. Went to high school here. Went off to college and then came back and married a local, then left again."

Derek's brown-eyed gaze drifted to her left ring finger. "I didn't realize you were married. You should have sent me off to talk to Mr. Hamill about construction." He felt a stirring of disappointment.

Joya spooned sugar into her coffee and laid the utensil down.

"I don't have a husband, and even if I had you'd still be talking to me. My grandmother left me in charge and with full authority to make decisions."

"Of course, that was somewhat chauvinistic of me to say."

Derek felt like applauding her. Diminutive as Joya was she was no pushover. He'd seen a more vulnerable side of her tonight which he liked, and he'd also realized there was more depth to her than he'd given her credit for.

"So why are you back in town?" Derek asked bluntly.

Those sultry gray eyes remained on him for quite some time as she debated how to answer.

"I was burnt out on my job and took a leave of absence. It made sense to come home."

"And you're here for how long?"

"Long enough to supervise the store's renovation

and make sure I'm happy with the changes. What about you? You've only recently returned to Flamingo Beach. Where are you living and how long will you be around? I'd hate for you to start work and then leave me high and dry with my property unfinished."

He'd left himself wide open for that.

"You have nothing to worry about."

That's all he would give her. That's all she deserved.

Joya took a sip of her tea. Her long lashes were lowered and it was impossible to see her eyes.

"You've rented a condo? A house? What?" she asked after a while.

"I live with my great-grandmother." He didn't know where this was going or why she wanted to know.

"I see."

Mario, the owner of the diner came bustling over.

"Hey Joya," he said, "You need anything? More pie? Some of mama's famous pasta? You tell Mario. It's on the house."

"Thank you, but I'm fine. Actually, I'm full," Joya said, giving Mario one of those wide smiles that made her gray eyes come to life.

The owner moved on to the next table and stood chatting up the occupants. This was pretty much his routine and the reason people enjoyed coming into Mario's. Black, white, tan or yellow you were always welcomed in his diner.

"So let's say your Mr. Shore agrees to refurbishing Nana's store. How soon could you start?" Joya asked.

Derek did some quick mental calculations. "The crew has at least three days work left at All About Flowers. They're currently laying floors and there's still painting to be done. The guys at the Vintage Place have walls to knock down, and then the owners, the Millards, want the windows replaced, so that may take a week or so. We could probably start in the next ten days."

"And you'd be heading up this crew?" Joya asked, her sculptured eyebrows coming together in a frown. "How long did you say you've been in construction?"

"I didn't say. But to answer your question, all my grown life."

It was really a half truth. Derek had always liked working with his hands and he'd done most of the work on his own condominium. He'd brought in electricians to handle the wiring and plumbers to take care of the pipes. Other then that he'd done it on his own.

"Hmmm."

What was that supposed to mean? Before he could analyze the sound, a female voice came from behind him.

"Derek!"

Sheena Grace. She would have to show her face now. As usual she was overdressed, especially for a weekday night. The outfit was ridiculous—pants that stopped above the ankle, wedge shoes with satin ribbons circled her ankles and a scooped-neck, chiffon blouse that reminded him of something women wore to bed.

"Hey, Sheena," Derek said, popping up—because it was expected of him—and sliding out of the banquette to greet her.

Sheena used that opportunity to wrap her arms around his neck and kiss him directly on the lips. When she finally broke the lip-lock, she said, "I haven't heard from you in a while." A finger reached out tracing a pattern around the emblem on his polo shirt. She was marking him as her territory and he did not appreciate it one bit.

Derek took a step back, successfully putting space between them. He captured Sheena's hand and placed it back at her side where it belonged.

"I've been busy. There's a lot going on."

"You're always busy. You don't ever make time for me," she whined as though there was a "them."

"Do you know Joya?" Derrick asked, turning back to the woman still seated at the table.

Sheena tossed a sulky look in Joya's direction. "I've seen her around."

"Then let me introduce you."

Both women pretended graciousness.

Mario's busboys were starting to pick up chairs and stack them on tables. That meant it was almost close to the witching hour, eleven, and boy, was Derek grateful.

"I've got to get home," Joya said, bailing him out and glancing at her watch pointedly. "Nice meeting you, Sheena. I'll see you at Quen and Chere's wedding."

Sheena's lower lip flapped open. "They invited you?"

"Yes, and I plan on being there."

Oh, boy, he hated cat fights, wanted no part of them.

"Ready?" Derek asked Joya, holding out his hand and helping her from the confining banquette. "Nice seeing you, Sheena. I'll be in touch."

Holding Joya's tiny hand in his, he walked with her to the exit.

The next evening the guild gathered in the back room of the quilt shop. Joya welcomed everyone and explained to those who hadn't heard why she was running things instead of Granny J. She had her own quilt work and she wanted to talk to the group about making commemorative quilts for the centennial.

Earlier that day Joya had managed to get someone to come in to repair the window that had been broken. Lionel and Greg had not had much success with Deborah and LaTisha, both had claimed to be elsewhere and the police were checking out their alibis.

Meanwhile, the two officers promised to patrol the Row more frequently while keeping an eye on Joya's Quilts in particular.

While Joya was somewhat uneasy remaining at the store after hours, she kept reminding herself that she was surrounded by a large number of women, and so relatively safe. The quilt makers were a diverse group of people, ranging in age from mid twenties to seniors in their eighties and nineties. They ran the gamut from professionals to stay-at-home moms. And they were all there for one purpose, the love of quilt-making.

When Joya was finished telling everyone about Granny J and her own quilt-making plan she added, "These commemorative quilts are another wonderful opportunity to put our town on the map and generate some revenue. If you're interested, the shop will take your quilts or pillows on consignment. We can showcase the town's history and you can make some money at the same time. I already have one client who wants a combination of family album and autograph book. He needs a fairly quick turnaround. Do I have takers?

Eileen Brown, the marketing manager at the *Flamingo Beach Chronicle* and one young mother's hand shot up.

"Who is the customer?" Eileen asked, "Anyone I know?"

"Derek Morse."

"Oooh!" the young mother said. "He's a fine-looking man."

"Down, girl," another woman hissed, rolling her eyes. "You already have yourself a husband, leave him for someone like me who's single."

That cracked the group up and they moved on to other gossip. Joya learned who'd taken up with whom and who was soon to be evicted. She heard who'd found a new job and who was expecting a baby.

When there was a lull in the gossip, Joya explained what Derek wanted. "I'll give both of you ladies his contact information at the end of this session and you can work out the particulars with him," she said. "I've agreed to help as well."

For what remained of the two hours, she worked on her quilt which was a version of the Tree of Life. Curious to see the others' designs, she wandered about admiring the blocks people were working on.

One woman had started a four-block version of the Poinsettia Feathered Star. She said it would be a gift to her daughter for Christmas. Another, fairly new to the process, was creating a classic four-block redwork wall hanging. Since the octagonal star centers required only beginner to intermediate machine skills this wouldn't be too difficult. The woman freely admitted that she'd taken up quilting as therapy. It soothed her soul as it had done for a lot of women through some of their worst crises.

At the end of the evening, Eileen Brown and the young woman who'd volunteered collected Derek's phone number and e-mail address. The group then made plans to meet again on Saturday morning, and everyone left.

Joya quickly began checking to make sure the windows were securely fastened and each access and exit locked. She made a quick call to the part-time worker, Portia Cortez, to make sure she was coming in tomorrow. Earlier she'd found her number in one of Granny J's books and left a message. Portia assured her she would be in. The backup plan would have been to lock up the store since she needed to be at the hospital tomorrow with Granny J throughout her surgery.

When Joya let herself out the front door, she felt her trepidation build. Anyone could be lying in wait in the shadows. She should have asked one of the women to remain with her while she closed up. She shone her flashlight across the walkway and carefully picked her way down.

"So how did it go? Did you find someone to make my quilt?"

The voice was familiar, male and too close to her ear for her liking.

"Oh, God, you startled me."

"I'm sorry," Derek said, touching her arm and making her whole body tingle. "I worked late and saw the light in the back room on, then I saw the number of cars out front and figured something was up. I decided to wait around, one of the women who left early told me the quilt guild was meeting. After what happened last evening I thought you might need an escort to your car."

"That was nice of you. Two women are interested in making your quilt. I gave them your information and asked them to get in touch with you."

Derek had hold of her arm by the elbow and together they came down the walkway slowly.

"Did they say what they would charge?" he asked.

"I told you I'd split it." An idea began to formulate. "Depending on how long it takes Gran to recuperate I might be able to work on some of it myself. That would help cut down the expense."

"I told you that wasn't necessary. I'm quite capable of paying for the whole thing myself."

Derek was one proud man. She couldn't imagine where he would find the money to pay for the type of commemorative quilt he wanted his great-grandmother to have. Construction workers didn't make enough money to afford customized quilts. At least not the kind of construction workers who lived with their relatives.

"Can I ask why you're being so resistant?" Joya asked. "What's so wrong with me splitting a gift with you?"

They'd almost reached her car. Derek held out his hand for her key. He used the remote to snap the doors open and then waited for Joya to get in.

"Belle's my folk," he said, "Not yours. This is my special gift. But if you want to work on the quilt, that I will accept."

"It'll go faster with three people on it," Joya said starting the car. "What's happening with my construction job?"

Derek stuck his head through the open window. "Are you in a hurry right now?"

She shook her head. "Not really. I checked on granny earlier. She's gone to bed. Tomorrow is her surgery."

"Let's pray everything goes well. If you haven't had dinner, join me," Derek said, "We can discuss what needs to be done, what it's going to cost and how long it will take."

"Shouldn't Preston Shore be telling me this?"

"Preston is a busy man. He told me to handle it and if we can come to an agreement then he'll draw up the paperwork."

She was hungry and this was business, Joya reminded herself. Not exactly a date.

"Where did you have in mind?"

"If the Catch-All sounds good you can meet me there."

"Okay." She started the vehicle up again. She was doing this because Granny J's store needed remodeling. She was not at all attracted to Derek Morse and never would be.

Chapter 8

The Catch-All was having one of those buffet-style deals, as much as you can eat for one set price. Even though it was late, the place attracted a fair share of families and young people out on a date.

Derek had just returned from the buffet line, his plate full to overflowing. The items he'd chosen were all healthy—plenty of greens, brown rice, catfish, chicken breasts and peas. He planned to wash them down with a huge glass of sweet tea.

Joya's own plate looked like the appetizer next to his. After the crawfish soup she'd been close to full so she'd had the shrimp and scallop dish served in garlic sauce with a little linguini on the side. Now she was beginning to regret going for the garlic.

She'd also noticed the looks they were getting. Speculative. Quizzical. They'd now been seen out two nights in a row. This could mean only one thing, the two of them were dating.

Joya waited until Derek had taken a large gulp of tea and it had settled. Her eyes fastened on his hands. Large hands. Clean hands. Hands that a lot of women wouldn't mind having on their bodies…

"Talk to me about the plans for renovation," she said, uneasy at how quickly her mind had drifted to sex. A not-uncommon thing when Derek was around her.

He unfolded one of the paper napkins, found a pen in the pocket of his shirt and began sketching.

"Here's what I propose. We knock out one of the walls and widen your porch area. It would give you room to put in a glider and several rocking chairs, giving the place a homier look, plus you would have a place to display more quilts.

"The showroom should be larger and airier. That drop ceiling needs to go. I'd put in a loft." Derek made a few deft strokes on the napkin. "This wall dividing the show room and the work room where the quilt guild meets—boom! Gone!"

"And where's the group supposed to meet?"

"They get together after hours for the most part, don't they?" He looked at her, waiting for her to concur.

"Yes, but on Saturdays, too."

"With a bigger showroom, the sewing machines and stuff they need would be off to the side. I'd create a corner, one huge alcove with lots of shelving and storage space. Personally I think if customers saw quilts being made on the premises it would drive business and give people a reason to custom-order."

Derek made a good point, but Joya wasn't sure she cared for the way he presented it, as if it were a done deal. As if he, and only he, had a say. Plus she wasn't sure Granny J would agree to such a drastic change. The old lady did tend to be set in her ways. Thoughts of her granny brought to mind the surgery scheduled for tomorrow. Joya prayed it would go well.

"No comments. You're not going to fight me?" Derek asked after swallowing his fish."

"How much is all of this going to cost?"

"Not as much as you think, plus it can be done quickly. It's not like you have to bring an architect in. I can take care of the design for you." He named a figure that made her blink once. "Basically we're talking about knocking down a couple of walls, putting in some shelving, raising the ceiling and building a loft."

"Sounds pretty expensive to me, and messy."

Derek finished up his meal and lined his knife and fork up on the side of his plate.

"Not messy if it's done properly. It will all be worth it. You'll see."

"Hey Derek, I hear your great-gran's having a party. Make sure me and Winston are invited."

Camille Lewis, the town gossip, was standing right over them. Joya hadn't even heard her come up.

Derek stood to greet the woman. Well brought up, Joya thought.

"Hi Camille, Nana Belle's made up her own list. I'm sure she'll invite the people she wants," he said diplomatically.

"You two have something going on?" Camille asked, eyeing Joya shrewdly.

"Business," Joya corrected, "This is a business meeting."

"Looks like monkey business to me."

"Camille!" Winston, Camille's husband's voice came from behind them. "We need to leave."

"In a minute."

"Now."

"Business, uh, so that's what you call it these days," Camille said, as her husband tugged on her arm. "Give my best to Granny J. Let her know I'm praying for her."

"I'll do that." Joya kept her expression neutral, at least she hoped she did. What Joya really wanted to do was strangle the annoying woman.

Camille finally left. By then Joya no longer had an appetite for dessert and said so. Derek signaled for the bill.

"You find the prospect of me and you out on a date that distasteful?" Derek joked.

Joya didn't want to hurt his feelings. Attracted to him or not, she just didn't see the point of starting something that she wasn't about to finish. Once Granny J was pronounced well enough to be on her own she was out of here, back to her old job. No point in leading Derek on. Why have him believe he stood a chance when he didn't? She was looking for a nice home in the suburbs, complete with two kids, the dog, the picket fence, the whole nine yards. She wanted to be home to raise those kids. She couldn't see Derek being in a position to give her that.

Joya threw some dollars on the table, her share of the bill.

"Keep your money," Derek said. "Since this is a business meeting Shore Construction can pay."

Was he being sarcastic or simply letting her know that he could afford to pay for their meal?

Better to be gracious and just accept. She picked

up her money, leaving a twenty behind. "How about I leave the tip?"

"I have that covered." He slid the bill back toward her.

Gentleman that he was, he walked her to her car.

"Thanks for dinner," Joya said, at the same time depressing the button on the remote lock.

"My pleasure. What time is your grandmother's surgery?"

Joya felt herself tear up; just thinking of Granny J under the knife made her weepy and that was not at all like her. "Early. I plan on being at the hospital at seven."

"You're keeping the store closed then?" Derek asked.

She hoped he hadn't caught on that she was trying her best not to let her emotions take over. "Not exactly. The student who works part-time can handle the morning activity."

"Your grandmother's going to be just fine," Derek said, the back of his hand grazing her cheek in an incredibly intimate gesture. Joya felt herself go warm all over. She gulped back a sob.

"I hope so. Now I'd better go. Morning comes around faster than you know it."

"That's true," Derek said, closing the space between them and enveloping her in a tight bear hug. He felt safe, even smelled safe.

His mouth pressed against hers in a chaste kiss that soon heated up and took on a life of its own. When he parted his lips, their tongues dipped, danced and melded. The heady scent of his soap filled her nostrils. Joya clung to him, enjoying the feeling of his rippling muscles under her hand and the searing kiss that was both exploratory and passionate.

Then good sense returned. What was she doing?

"Uhhh," she said, "Uhhh," wiggling out of his hold. "I've got to get home."

Derek's arms fell to his sides. Joya used that time to put several inches between them. Her lips still tingled and felt raw. She was wired and jumpy. They stared at each other for what seemed an eternity.

"I suppose I shouldn't have done that," Derek eventually said. "But I'm glad I did."

"I didn't exactly stop you."

Joya fled for her car. "Thanks again for dinner," she said hurriedly.

"You're most welcome."

She closed the vehicle door quickly and put the key in the ignition, starting it up.

Derek was still standing there staring. He raised his hand in a half salute. She wiggled her fingers at him and quickly backed the automobile out.

She should never have allowed this happen. And she didn't plan on it happening again.

* * *

Next morning, a perky nurse came bouncing into the waiting room where Joya sat restlessly flipping through a magazine. While relatives of other patients paced, ignoring the no-cell-phone policy, Joya tuned out the snippets of conversation and tried not to think of Derek's kiss. And what a kiss it had been!

"How's my grandmother?" Joya asked, putting the magazine aside and heading off the nurse who was there looking for someone other than her.

"Stable. She did great. A bit woozy from the anesthesia but otherwise fine."

"When can I see her?"

"As soon as she's fully awake."

Joya sent a silent prayer up to God for bringing Granny J through this. It would have been devastating had anything happened to her grandmother.

The nurse was already busy talking to another family. Now would be a good time to step out of the waiting room, call the shop and check with Portia to see how things were going. Joya also badly needed some fresh air. Despite her vow to go straight home to bed last night, that had not happened. She'd lain awake thinking of Derek Morse and his kiss. She should never have allowed that to happen, and she promised herself for the umpteenth time it wouldn't happen again.

She slid into a surprisingly crowded elevator and rode it down to the lobby. The grounds surrounding the sprawling building with its many annexes were lush, well-tended and had the stamp of a landscape architect's work. Every blade of grass was perfectly arranged.

A profusion of exotic flowers and shrubbery made you think you were strolling through a serene park with plenty of walkways and hidden oases. Joya strolled down an impatien-lined path, palm trees swaying overhead. She plopped down on the first bench she spotted and got her cell phone out.

"Hey Portia, how's it going?"

"I'm glad you called. It's a little on the slow side. Mrs. Williams wanted to come by for her quilt, but I can't find it."

"Did you look under the counter where the register is? It's in the same brown shopping bag that it was handed to me in."

"Hold on a second."

Joya waited while Portia went off to look for the bag. Eileen Brown had handed her the finished quilt before she'd left the shop last night. Joya had put it on a shelf under the register for safekeeping. And Eileen had also asked her to make sure and collect the balance owed by Molly Williams, and to take the store's share before writing her a check.

"Uh, Joya," the student's voice trembled.

"Yes, Portia."

"The bag's there but the quilt has big cuts in it. It looks like someone took scissors to it or a cat went to work and had happy feet."

"What! It was in perfect condition when Eileen handed it to me. I took it out of the bag to admire the Princess Feather pattern."

"Well it's not in perfect condition any more. What should I do if Mrs. Williams comes by?"

"Stall her," Joya said quickly, wondering what the heck was going on. "Fib a little. Tell her Eileen hasn't come by with the quilt yet. When I get back I'll take a look at the quilt and see if it's repairable."

"Trust me, it's not. I have to go now. Two customers just walked in."

Joya shoved the phone back into her purse and sat with her head in her hands, thinking. She'd scrutinized that quilt last evening, admiring the workmanship and complimenting Eileen for the superb job she'd done. There had been no tears, rips or signs of destruction.

She'd been down here almost half an hour. Time to get back to Granny J.

But Granny was still not in her room when Joya poked her head in.

"Your grandmother's still not back," the elderly

woman who was Granny J's roommate said. "I asked the nurse if there was a problem. She said 'no.' Seems like a long time to be gone though."

Joya wondered if there was a complication that the nurse had failed to mention to her. Maybe it was time to find someone who could give her answers.

She approached the nurses' station and waited patiently for someone to acknowledge her. Finally one of the nurses broke away from what she was doing.

"Can I help you?"

"I'd like to speak to Dr. Benjamin if I may. He performed surgery on my grandmother and she's still not back in her room. I need someone who can tell me what's going on."

"Just a moment," the nurse said, turning away and going off to pick up a phone that she spoke into quietly.

"Dr. Benjamin will be right up," she returned to say. "You can wait comfortably in the lounge, and I'll get you when he's here."

Joya thanked her and returned to the waiting area, hoping this wouldn't take too long. Once she was assured Granny J was on the road to recovery she needed to get to the store and find out what had happened with that quilt.

Twenty minutes later the nurse stood at the entrance beckoning to her. Dr. Ben, still in his scrubs, waited in front of the nurses' station.

"Your grandmother did well," he hastened to assure Joya before going on to explain in layman's terms how he'd unblocked her arteries. "Sometimes seniors take a bit longer to recover from anesthesia. I recommended she remain in recovery until she's fully alert. Take off and do what you need to do, then come back and visit later. We'll contact you if we need you."

"You're telling me the absolute truth?" Joya asked, searching Dr. Ben's face for evidence that he was not being straight with her.

Dr. Benjamin squeezed her shoulder. "I'm telling you the absolute truth. Go do what you need to do. Your grandmother will be here waiting."

"Thanks, Doctor Ben."

Assured that her grandmother was resting comfortably, Joya made the journey across town as quickly as possible running every amber light she encountered. There were a few browsing customers in the store when she arrived so she kept herself busy checking the supply room and the inventory, making note of stock that was running low so that she could talk to Granny J about reordering.

Finally there was a lull in business and she was able to speak with Portia.

"How did it go with Molly Williams?"

"I was able to delay her coming by," Portia said. "She wasn't real happy. I told her you weren't here and I didn't feel comfortable collecting money from her since I didn't know how much she owed. I told her you would call her later."

"That was quick thinking on your part. Where's the damaged quilt?"

"In the bag." Portia bent over and found the brown paper bag where she'd stashed it. She placed it on the counter. "Take a look. Tell me what you think."

Joya reached inside to remove the comforter that had been carefully folded. She shook the material out. Sure enough, the quilt had huge gashes in it and looked like a maniac had gone to work on it with a pair of scissors. It was beyond repair.

Okay, the first step was to call Eileen Brown, the woman who'd made it. Joya reached for the phone. After a few rings, Eileen's machine came on. Joya left a message.

"Molly Williams will probably be calling you soon," Portia reminded her.

"Until I hear back from Eileen I'm going to have to ask you to hold her off. Just say I can't be reached, and that I'll get back to her as soon as I can."

"What are you going to do?" Portia asked. "What *can* you do?" The college student's voice wobbled and her jerky movements indicated how nervous she was.

"Talk to Eileen and verify that she gave me the quilt in good condition. Then ask her to take a look and see if any of it is salvageable. Find out how long it will take to make another one."

"You know the answer to that."

"Yes, I think I do, but if I enlist the help of the guild we may be able to turn another one out in record time. It'll cost me, but it's better than having the store's reputation ruined."

The phone rang and both women reached for it. Portia was quicker.

"Hello." She listened for a bit before covering the mouthpiece and holding the receiver out. "It's for you. It's your supervisor from L.A. International."

Joya felt her mouth go dry. This could mean only one thing; the airline wanted her back at work.

It couldn't come at a worse time. In addition to everything else, she probably had a life-changing decision to make.

Taking a deep breath, and preparing herself for the worst, Joya took the phone.

Chapter 9

"Hello, this is Joya." Joya sucked in a breath, waited for the next shoe to drop.

"This is Sara Watkins, your supervisor. I thought I would check in with you and see how you're coming along."

"It's not been an easy few months," Joya said and waited.

A long pause followed. A palpable pause then finally. "I can't extend your leave past the time we agreed to. L.A. International has just signed a contract with the military for several charters. We need everybody we can get back. We're actually canceling leaves of absence."

"How long do I have?"

"According to my paperwork, at the most another couple of weeks," Sara said, sounding more friendly. She wasn't a bad person, she just had a job to do.

"And then?"

"After that you'll have to resign."

Bam!

Joya was close to hyperventilating. It was ultimatum time and she'd just been given one.

"My grandmother just underwent major surgery," she pleaded. "I am the only person she has. At least, her only relative in the state of Florida."

"I wish I could help," Sara said, "But you've already extended your leave three times. A personal leave became a hardship leave and then it became an emergency leave. You've been gone over six months. L.A. International needs you back."

"And if I tender my resignation?" Joya asked.

"At least you'd be eligible for rehire. You've got eight years seniority, hardly something to sneeze at."

"I understand. I'm at the hospital right now. I'll have to get back to you."

For a long time after she hung up, Joya sat holding the phone in her hand.

Decisions. She'd have to make a few, but regardless, she would do the right thing by Granny J. Without her she would be nowhere.

The work at All About Flowers was moving along right on schedule and Derek was pleased. Bringing the job in on time meant a bonus for him, money he planned on using either to fix up Nana Belle's house or invest in her party.

As he stood on the top of the ladder looking down at new wooden floors the crew had just laid, Preston Shore walked in.

"Hey Preston, have a minute?" Derek called to the contractor from his perch. "I want to talk to you about starting work at Joya's Quilts."

Preston removed his hard hat and squinted up at Derek. He'd come by to inspect the workmanship at the shop, and judging by his wide smile he seemed happy with the results.

"I thought I gave it the go-ahead? Once we finish up here we were going to start work on Joya's." He waved expansively at the interior of the flower shop. "Great job, guys."

Derek, realizing one of the owners, Chet Rabinowitz, was listening to every word, slowly came down the ladder and faced Preston.

"It's almost lunchtime anyway. How about you

and me grab a quick sandwich and we can talk about Joya's?"

"Quills is right next door," Preston suggested. "Afterward we can see how work is progressing at the Vintage Place."

"Hallelujah!" Chet exclaimed, confirming he was eavesdropping. "Granny J finally agreed to fix up that old place, and about time I say."

Preston didn't dignify it with a comment. He said to the crew still working, "Carry on with what you're doing and break for lunch as scheduled. Derek and I are stepping out."

Derek waited until they were on their way over before bringing up Joya's again.

"I'd like to start work on the quilt shop next week. It should only take a couple of men to finish up the flower shop."

"Ms. Joya have anything to do with this sudden enthusiasm?"

Derek stabbed an index finger at him and cut his eyes. "How many times have I told you I'm not looking to get involved? The woman is beautiful, but she's high-maintenance and quite bossy. She would be looking to fix me. I like myself just the way I am."

"Whatever you say."

Derek decided to ignore his friend's pointed smirk. Preston was acting like he knew something

Derek didn't. Derek allowed him to enter Quill's first. They sauntered past the stationary and to the back where the café was and looked around for seats.

All the bistro tables were taken, and even the eight tables on the outdoor patio were full. A harried waitress weighted down by a heavy tray brushed by them as several patient customers craned their heads. Just then two men slid off stools at the counter.

"Better move quickly," Preston said, dashing over. "You snooze, you lose."

They grabbed the vacated seats and menus were quickly slapped down in front of them. The owner was also the chef and this might have added to the confusion. After some time a put-upon waitress poured them water and the men made their selections. Deciding the place was either short-staffed or hadn't anticipated a crowd, they prepared for a long wait.

It was an interesting group at lunch, hardly a local to be found. Derek remembered a time when the only tourists that sleepy Flamingo Beach ever saw were families from up north looking to rent cabins, fish and stroll the boardwalk. Times were indeed changing.

"I'm going to need a deposit from Joya's Quilts before we get started," Preston said. "You know the routine. Collect enough to buy supplies and some. We'll need either Joya or Granny J to sign the paperwork stating what they've agreed to have done."

Derek squinted at Preston. "I thought you were handling the administrative end."

"No, you are. You're in training. These are all the things that will be expected of you when you own and run your own construction company." Preston winked at him. "And by the way, you can start your negotiations now. Young Joya just walked in and she has one of her employees with her."

Despite not wanting to gawk, Derek swiveled his stool to stare in the direction Preston was looking. Joya stood at the entrance of the café with a young girl with waist-length braids at her side. They looked around for an available table.

"Food's here. Sorry it took me so long," the waitress said, slapping down Preston's burger and fries and Derek's turkey sandwich with coleslaw on the side. "We're short-staffed."

Derek stared at his food. He didn't want to talk contracts now. The woman was there to have lunch. Preston was being conniving and trying to push them together. Well it wouldn't work. He'd slipped earlier that week and kissed her, but, hell, she'd looked so good. Can't blame a guy for reacting like any healthy red-blooded guy would. But it couldn't happen again. From now on his dealings with Joya Hamill would be kept strictly professional.

As Derek finished his turkey sandwich, he and

Preston discussed the job at the Flamingo Beach Spa and Resort that they were bidding on. Preston wanted it badly, but Derek wasn't so sure. He had the feeling the resort people would be bears to work for. But the money was good.

"This developer Rowan James is buying up land like crazy," Preston said. "Last I heard he bought that prime piece of real estate at the end of the boardwalk. Some say he's going to create an indoor mall, one of those super malls with movie theaters, restaurants and nightclubs. The town is violently opposed to it and petitions are already circulating."

"I see both sides," Derek said. "We're talking mall here. This is the kind of project that will change the face of Flamingo Beach, and not necessarily for the better. It will bring in money for the city, but at the same time it's going to attract a lot of hustlers. Anything money-making does."

"I'm thinking revenue," Preston countered. "People drive to Pelican Island if they want to see a current movie. Only in Flamingo Beach would a cinema open only in the evenings and the same show run for a month. We're not at all forward-thinking. We have Mayor Rabinowitz to blame for that. The money our citizens shell out should be spent right here."

"A nightclub is going to attract some undesirable types," Derek cautioned. "Even gangs. When you get a party crowd, there's excessive drinking, drugs and crime."

"Jeez, Derek you're beginning to sound like our parents." Preston gave Derek a friendly poke with his finger.

It was a sobering thought, since Derek's parents were long gone. Both had literally died from overwork. It was another reason he was determined to be his own boss and call his own shots. He planned on living to a ripe old age. His retirement was going to be exactly that: a time when he put his feet up and didn't have to worry about money.

By an unspoken agreement they removed bills from their wallets and slapped them down. Joya and her companion were now seated at a table in the middle of the room. Preston, of course, chose to take the long route out. He passed Joya's table and slowed down.

"How's your grandmother?" he asked.

Joya used a napkin to wipe her mouth. "She came out of the operation just fine. How are you, Preston, Derek?"

How was he? His body was telling him he was very happy to see her. He just hoped she couldn't tell.

"Great. Preston and I were just discussing starting work on your place. Does next Monday sound good to you?"

"The sooner the better. Business is picking up and by the time the centennial celebrations roll around it should be even better. Granny's store needs to be a showplace by then."

"You two should talk," Preston said. "Derek, you stop by later with the paperwork and work out the details about what needs doing."

Damn Preston. He'd just put him in a spot, one that it would be hard to wiggle out of. He would kill him when he got him outside.

"I'll come by right before closing time," Derek said since he had no choice.

"Tomorrow might be better," Joya said, those huge gray eyes clouding over. "I'm leaving early today. I'm going to the hospital to check on Gran."

"Saturday will work just as well. Won't it, Derek?"

"Sure will."

Outside, Preston said to Derek, "What's with you? Here's this fine woman who's single, smart and in shape, and you drag your feet. Man, I'd be jumping all over her."

Derek snorted. "I have my priorities, and I don't want to get off track. Nana's house comes first. Until it gets fixed, and I have my own construction company up and running, romance has to wait."

"Who's talking romance?" Preston lobbed back. "I'm talking getting laid."

"Plenty of that around for the taking. If I were looking for an activity partner I'd be all over Sheena Grace."

Preston threw his hands in the air. "Whatever."

They headed into the Vintage Place. Derek didn't think Preston would give up, but for now the conversation had been tabled.

For the rest of the day, he concentrated on Chet's leaking skylights and water-stained ceiling. At the end of the day most of what needed to be done was done. Derek assigned three men to come in during the weekend to take care of the baseboards, complete the painting and replace the lighting fixtures. Then on Monday the crew would be ready to take on Joya's Quilts.

"I'm going home," Derek said to Preston when his boss asked him to a happy hour. There was a bathroom at Belle's that needed his attention. The tub, washbasin and fixtures needed replacing. He planned to stop at the hardware store first before joining Nana Belle for supper. Repairing that house had become his second job.

On a Friday evening, Harry's Hardware wasn't too crowded. Derek was able to pick up the items he needed and get out of there in record time.

This time Belle heard him before he could put his key in the lock.

"That you, hon?" she called in her croaky smoker's voice.

"Yes, it's me."

"We've been holding mail for you," her aide Mari said. "The mailman made us sign for it."

Mari was no lightweight. Derek could hear the floorboards creaking as she left Nana Belle's room and made her way out.

Derek had had all of his mail forwarded to him from Chicago. For the most part it was all junk, but if a signature was required it had to be important.

Mari waved an official-looking white envelope at him. Derek took it from her, glanced at the sender's address, frowned and set it on the coffee table to be dealt with later. He couldn't imagine what his old company wanted with him.

"Aren't you going to open it?" Mari nudged. "Belle and I have been wondering what's so important that it would require a signature."

"I'll get to it later. How did my favorite lady do today?"

"She's been smoking non-stop but that's nothing new."

"Has she eaten?"

"I got her to swallow maybe a couple of tablespoons of grits and she did drink a nutritional milkshake."

"She'll need to eat dinner. I'm counting on you."

"Stop talking about me," Nana croaked from her back room. "I'm still alive. If you have something to say you might as well say it to my face."

"Okay, I'm on my way," Derek said, heading down the hallway.

The one thing he'd learned was that it didn't pay to back off when Nana became nasty or challenging. Best to face her head-on or she would just continue to bully you until she got her way.

As he got closer to Nana's room the acrid smell of stale tobacco smoke lodged in his throat. Although his stomach turned, Derek tried not to gag.

"How's the most beautiful woman in the world?" he asked, planting a kiss on one of Nana's sunken cheeks while trying not to inhale that nasty cigarette smell that clung to her clothes.

"One step away from death. What's going on down the boardwalk? There's been all kinds of equipment going back and forth."

Derek explained what he'd heard.

"Shopping mall. Did you say shopping mall? Why does Flamingo Beach need a shopping mall? We've survived almost one hundred years without it, so why do we need one now?"

"A lot of the town's folks are asking that same question, Nana. Miriam Young, the 'Flip-flop Momma,' who Solomon Rabinowitz stole the votes from in the last election, started a petition. There's a town meeting planned."

"I want to go," Belle surprised him by saying. "This isn't the first time some developer came in proposing to change this town, and it won't be the last. When's this meeting?"

Derek and Mari exchanged glances. This was the first time in months Nana Belle had expressed an interest in leaving the house. Normally the little sun porch at the side of her room was as far as she went. She was content to sit there for hours, staring at the action on the boardwalk and taking naps in between.

"We'll see, Nana," Derek said, trying to pacify her. "Let's have dinner before I go to work."

Mari left them to get Belle's tray and to bring Derek his dinner.

"Humph!" Belle said, lighting up yet another cigarette and blowing a smoke ring. "Who'd you say sent you that letter?"

"My old employer. I haven't opened it yet."

She exhaled again, creating another ring. "They want you to come back to work?"

"I don't think so. Last I knew they were still laying off."

The company that Derek had worked for as an engineer had been cutting back like crazy. They'd laid off hundreds of people. He would probably have been one of the last to go, but he'd seen it as a great opportunity to do something different. Derek had volunteered to take a severance package, money he could use to start up his own business.

Mari was back with Nana's tray. She'd put Derek's plate on it. "Where shall I put this?" she asked.

"Give it to me."

Mari handed his plate to him. The utensils that were folded into a napkin were put on the nightstand.

"You say the blessing, Nana," Derek said, bowing his head and closing his eyes.

Belle recited the words that were a tradition, as she had done for almost one hundred years. Derek silently added his own thanks. In the whole crazy scheme of things he had a lot to be grateful for. Life had been good.

Three hours later, he'd pulled most of the bathroom apart. Deciding to throw in the towel, so to speak, Derek poured himself a beer and took the letter to the back porch to read it. Nana was already asleep and Mari, patient soul that she was, was relaxing in the privacy of her room.

Derek's whole body hurt. He sat on the glider enjoying the darkness, legs stretched out in front of him. After taking a slug of beer, he set the bottle on the table next to him.

For some insane reason Joya Hamill kept popping

into his mind, and he couldn't seem to shake her. The crazy thing was he kept remembering their kiss and the feel of her slender body pressed against his. She'd responded to his kiss with passion and not like some dead fish. And he kept wondering what it would be like to sleep with her, though there was fat chance of that ever happening. Joya was not for him.

Derek finally rose to flip the light on. The mosquitoes buzzing around the lit bulb and the noise of waves crashing against the pilings were all too familiar. These were the sounds he'd gotten used to. While certainly not big city sounds they were soothing in their own way. They helped him get to sleep at night.

He removed the crumpled envelope from his pocket and tapped it against his knee. His instincts told him the contents could change his life. Better just get it over with and open the thing and find out.

Derek tore one end open and removed an official-looking piece of paper bearing the company logo. For years he'd gotten used to seeing Norcross and McPhinney and never once given it another thought. But now—his jaw muscles working, Derek quickly scanned the letter.

Dear Derek:

I tried reaching you but your phone number was disconnected. Since you left no forwarding number I've decided to write. We've made some changes at Norcross and McPhinney. I'm now the vice president of your old department.

I need a committed, loyal team as we move forward. Someone with your experience in project management would certainly be welcomed back. You are well regarded and perhaps you would consider coming aboard as a consultant. Get back to me and we'll talk.

Best,
John Eldridge
Vice President Operations

John, his buddy and probably the only person in his old company who knew how truly committed he'd been to their cause. John knew how much time and sacrifice he'd put into the organization. It had cost him his wife and the life that Derek had grown used to. Now John was in a position to offer him work. Consultants were generously paid.

An offer like this one was not something a smart man dismissed without some consideration. He would give it some thought.

It was a world of meetings and politics. A world that required proper dress, where jeans were worn only on Fridays, and traffic-filled highways created their own stress.

John had mentioned consulting. Maybe he could consult from right here. It was done all the time.

Technology made anything possible.

Chapter 10

Joya finished writing her resignation letter and set down her pen. She was emotionally drained and a little bit scared. But it was done with. Over. Now all she needed to do was go to the post office and send the letter certified mail. The thought that she was now officially unemployed made her lightheaded and dizzy. She'd just severed her ties with Los Angeles and left her future to chance.

She couldn't really blame L.A. International for taking such a firm stand. She'd been away from her job for six months and then she'd asked to have her leave extended. There were other flight attendants who'd applied for leaves of absence and had been turned down.

While it was a tough decision, it was the only one she could make. Family mattered more than any job, and she planned on being with her grandmother through the recuperation process. Joya had no intention of abandoning her namesake when she needed her most.

Still, there was something frightening about no longer having a job to go back to. It had been a while since she'd drawn a check from L.A. International, but it was still comforting to know that she could if she returned to L.A. Another flight attendant had moved into her condo and was paying her rent. He could be talked into taking over the lease permanently since it was such a good deal.

Earlier, Joya had broken the news to Molly Williams that her quilt wasn't quite ready. That was, of course, a big fat lie. To compensate Molly for the delay, Joya had had to adjust the price by twenty percent. And then Lionel and Greg came by with no news. They hadn't had one single lead. She'd told them about the shredded quilt and that had been duly noted. They'd left to talk to Portia and see if she knew something she wasn't saying.

When midday rolled around she was ecstatic. Derek still hadn't shown up but, determined to enjoy her weekend she closed the store anyway. He could talk to her on Monday.

Now she left the dining room to throw open the French doors and get an unobstructed view of the ocean. Still feeling off, she pressed her forehead against the glass and reflected. Here she was at thirty-three, single with no viable prospects in sight. Others were buying houses and planning families and she was homeless and without a job.

She was feeling sorry for herself, she decided. Enough already. What she needed to do was get out where there was life. The sun was still high in the sky and the umbrellas still sheltered people. She'd mail her letter on Monday. Maybe she could coax Emilie into taking a bike ride down the boardwalk with her.

Joya picked up the phone and punched in Emilie's number.

"I was just thinking about calling you," Emilie said, sounding as if she'd been napping.

"Feel like taking a bike ride on the boardwalk?" Joya asked.

"I'd rather roller-skate, better exercise and we won't have to worry about parking bikes someplace."

"Good idea. I need to burn up some calories. I'll meet you at the guardhouse in twenty minutes. Maybe we'll skate toward the lighthouse."

"Twenty minutes it is."

That gave her just enough time to throw on a pair of shorts and a T-shirt. She found her skates in the back of the closet where she had tossed them, grabbed her backpack, put on flip-flops and took off.

Emilie was waiting at the agreed-upon place in her tight shorts and a T-back top. She had a fanny pack belted around her waist and a cap with the bill pulled low over her eyes. Her ponytail swished as she dabbed sunblock on her creamy shoulders.

"Ready?" she asked, removing her sneakers and tying the laces so that the shoes hung around her neck like a necklace.

"Ready," Joya answered, stepping out of her flip-flops and into her skates. She shoved her slippers in her backpack and whizzed by the security guard who looked at them as though they were crazy. The guardhouse, a relatively new addition to Flamingo Place, had been built as more upscale clientele moved in. There'd been an outbreak of petty thefts and the tenants and owners had pushed for a gated community.

They skated down the boardwalk, passing everything from seniors reading the newspapers to vendors hawking anything short of their sisters. Mothers pushed strollers with gurgling babies, elderly men played chess and tourists outfitted in skimpy bikinis wandered in and out of stores as if they owned them.

It felt good having the wind on her cheeks and inhaling the smell of brine and cotton candy. It felt good working muscles that she hadn't in a long time. Emilie was way ahead of her, hair streaming behind, winding her way around people and vendors and garnering the attention of every male.

The exercise was slowly helping clear Joya's head. She'd made the right choice by resigning, and she should look at it as a new beginning, an opportunity to do something with the degree that she had not utilized. Or maybe she could try something new. She'd always wanted to be an interior designer. With all the new construction, she just might get her shot. It was certainly worth having a discussion with Emilie since she had the contacts.

Emilie had slowed down and was bending over, hands on her knees taking deep breaths. Joya came alongside her.

"We can walk the rest of the way," she suggested.

"Only if we roller-skate back."

Roller skates were exchanged for sneakers and flip-flops. Joya tucked her skates into her backpack and Emilie wore hers around her neck like a Hawaiian lei. Ahead of them the lighthouse was a tall white column, silhouetted against a blue sky.

"Do you really believe it's haunted?" Emilie asked.

Joya's laughter trilled. "It makes for a good story. Romance with a tragic ending seems to appeal to most. It's like the old Romeo and Juliet story except this lovesick woman jumps through the window when she finds out her man died in a shipwreck. They're said to roam the place calling to each other."

"Ohhh!" Emilie shuddered, "That gives me the chills. The kids should have fun though. They're turning the lighthouse into a haunted house for the centennial celebrations."

A stream of tourists were paying the one-dollar fee a vagrant was charging to enter the building.

"Look, old Billy is at it again," Joya said, "He's been doing this forever. I bet you he has a mighty fine nest egg away tucked away somewhere."

"Hey, it's a capitalist world. Race you to the water."

Like two children, they flung their backpacks and roller skates on the sand and raced toward the bay.

After ten minutes of frolicking, Emilie sank down on the damp sand.

"So, what's up with you and Derek Morse?"

Joya rolled her eyes. "Derek and I are all about business. Shore Construction's renovating Gran's store. Derek and I are working out the details to make that happen."

"He's something of a mystery and yummy, huh?"

"Not in my book."

Emilie flipped her ponytail and tugged on the end. "You don't sound like you like him?"

"He's all right, just not particularly ambitious. He seems content working construction. The guy's smart enough and personable enough, but he lives with his grandmother. Why would any grown man live with a relative unless he didn't have his act together?"

"Things aren't always what they seem. He could be saving his money or helping out Belle. Maybe he's just content with where he is in life. There's something to be said about that. Most of us aren't."

"I suppose."

"But you've seen him two nights in row?" Emilie said, eyebrows arched.

"It's business and I'm seeing him again tonight. He's coming over later with paperwork and to collect a check."

"Hmmm. That would make three nights in a row."

"Stop being a wise ass." Clearly time to change the subject. "What's happening with you? The last I heard you were actively looking for a date to go to Quen and Chere's wedding."

Emilie stuck her legs straight out ahead of her. "I have my eye on someone, but he's affiliated with the resort so I'm reluctant to ask. If things get sticky it could be awkward. You still shopping?"

"Yup."

"Why don't you ask Derek Morse?"

"No." Emilie had clearly lost her mind.

"Betcha he cleans up well."

"No."

But even as Joya said the vehement no, she realized the wedding was only a week away and she'd need to find a date soon. No way was she going by herself. In a pinch Richard Dyson, the owner of Dyson Limousine Service could be counted on. Dickie never said no, to an attractive woman or free food. But then she'd have to deal with the consequences, and she wasn't that desperate yet.

Joya rose and began brushing the damp sand off her clothing. "If we're forking out a buck to get into the lighthouse, we might as well get it out of the way," she said.

"I changed my mind. Too many tourists. Let's walk down the beach a bit and roller-skate home."

"Going to tonight's jam?" Joya asked as they started back.

"I think so. You?"

"Yes, after I check on Gran. Look for me, I'll get there eventually."

The weekly Twilight Jam session featuring local talent was something of a tradition. It gave the townsfolk a place to be on a Saturday night and drew a good-sized crowd.

As they started back, Emilie kicked the incoming surf and frolicked through the water. Joya joined her. Emilie's mood was easily contagious.

"You have to go back to work soon, don't you?" Her friend had to ask, reopening that can of worms.

"Uh-uh."

"What does uh-uh mean?"

"I'm officially unemployed."

"What?"

Joya explained why she'd been forced to resign.

"What are you going to do for work?" Emilie asked, looking at Joya carefully for a reaction.

What was she going to do for work?

"I still have some savings. While Gran's recuperating I'll run the store and decide whether I'm staying on in Flamingo Beach or not. Maybe I'll try my hand at interior design. I've always had a good eye for fabric and color. I was going to ask you if anyone at the resort needed an assistant. I work cheap."

"I'll check around," Emilie said. "You're a hard worker. Hey, isn't that Derek coming toward us?"

Joya snapped to attention. "Where?" Hearing his name had the strangest effect on her. Her whole body now tingled.

"Over there." Emilie pointed to the boardwalk where a long-limbed, dark-skinned man jogged.

Joya squinted in that direction. "Your eyesight's great."

"It's hard to miss anyone who looks like that, not with that body." Emilie's voice had gone all high and she swept several wisps of hair off her face. "Tell me you're not just a teenie-weenie bit interested in him? The guy is a walking billboard for sex."

"He's not my type," Joya said tightly.

Emilie gave her a sideways look. "Okay, since he's not your type maybe I'll ask him to escort me to the wedding."

"Didn't you say you had someone else in mind?"

"Yes, but…"

Emilie was already racing toward the steps leading up to the boardwalk. She plopped down at the top and quickly put on her roller skates then pushed off in the direction that Derek was jogging. Joya's choice was either to follow or to head home.

By the time she caught up, Derek was jogging in place as Emilie circled him. A damp T-shirt clung to his broad chest and stretched across his washboard abs. Rivulets of sweat ran down his face and settled in the crevices around his mouth. He was breathing hard.

"Emilie Woodward," Joya heard Emilie say. "I met you and Preston Shore when you guys put in a bid for those waterfront villas."

Derek gave Emilie a slow, appraising smile. "Of

course I remember you. How could I forget? Love the more casual look."

Emilie preened and made another wide circle, pushing out her already impressive boobs. She was working it, making sure Derek got a good view of her cleavage, short-shorts and long, long legs. Her curly red hair fanned out behind her. She was larger than life and sexy to boot. Joya felt like an ugly little gnome beside her. Derek up until now had still not acknowledged her existence. She would not be ignored.

"Hello, Derek. You didn't show up today. How come?" she asked.

"Hey, Joya, girl is that you?" Derek's eyes lit up as if he recognized her for the first time. "I had no idea you were the athletic type."

He had stopped running in place and was doing a series of stretches and bends. He had this incredulous expression on his face.

"I was going to call you later and apologize," he added. "We ran into some problems at the Vintage Place, one of the guys hit a pipe and by the time the mess got sorted out you'd closed up." He tossed her another of those narrow-eyed looks as if he couldn't believe it was her. "I had no idea you roller-skated. Do you run?"

"Sometimes."

"Well, well." Derek placed both hands on his hips,

looking her over while Emilie continued to skate circles around them.

"I need to get home," Emilie said abruptly.

"What's the hurry?" Joya asked. Emilie seemed suddenly impatient to get going. She hadn't mentioned needing to be anywhere before.

She made a huge production of glancing at her watch. "I completely forgot about my hair appointment. See you later at the jam."

Off she whizzed, red hair creating a curtain behind her, leaving Joya to face Derek. Alone.

Chapter 11

"Are you in that much of a hurry?" Derek asked as if sensing she was about to bolt.

"Uh…"

"I've got the paperwork you need to sign in my truck."

"But I don't have my checkbook with me. Won't you need your deposit?" she argued.

"One of two things can happen," Derek said, seemingly unperturbed. "I can pick up the check later or you can drop it off."

There wasn't an excuse in the world she could give without being rude. She couldn't just walk away from him especially not if she wanted work to start Monday.

"Okay, let's get it over with. I'll drop off the deposit later if you don't mind."

"Or I can pick it up. Whichever is easier for you," Derek countered.

"I'll stop by your house."

In such close quarters Joya could smell the musk coming off him. It wasn't an unpleasant scent, and she tried to blink away the erotic vision of that hard, muscular body lying on top of her. Derek had runners' legs, muscles bunching in all the right places, and biceps that most men would kill for. She couldn't seem to come up with a response and she couldn't get his naked body out of her head.

If she allowed him to stop by her place who knew how that might end? One little kiss had gone to her head. It couldn't happen again. She couldn't risk it. Better to drop the check off at his home. She'd ring the doorbell, hand it to him and be on her way.

Derek pointed to someplace up the boardwalk. "Belle's house is off to the right, but I suppose you know that. Just let me know what time you'll be by. I'd hoped to catch the Twilight Jam."

"Me, too, after I go home, shower, change and visit Granny J at the hospital. Will seven be okay? The musicians usually don't start playing until eight."

Derek tilted his head to the side as if contemplating something. "Why don't you and I go together?"

"Um… Okay, sure."

She hadn't been able to come up with an excuse quickly enough. And truthfully, she wanted to find out more about the man. He was a heck of a lot more complicated than she'd given him credit for, but he was good company. Joya's conscience warred with her. Would she be misleading him, letting him believe he stood a chance? No, he was just being friendly, she decided, and she could be friendly back.

"Great. You bring a blanket to sit on and I'll bring a nice bottle of wine." He tapped her on the shoulder.

So much for stereotypes, she'd had him pegged as a beer drinker. No denying at glance number one there'd been chemistry between them, and more sparks than an electrical fire. In Derek's presence Joya felt edgy and wired. While words usually came easily, when he was around she was rendered damn close to inarticulate. She turned into a teenager again, awkward and unsure of herself. He was way too virile.

Together they started down the boardwalk, Joya trying her best to ignore the knowing looks and muttered speculation, often loud enough for them to hear. Every now and then they stopped to acknowledge someone they knew. She'd bet phones were ringing all over town. Some probably already had them married off.

Just wait until they showed up at tonight's jam session, then the whole of Flamingo Beach would have them sleeping together. She couldn't let that bother her. A lot worse had been said of her in the past. She'd been called all kinds of names when she'd left Quen. It had been said she'd left him for the town stud, and when that had failed to prove true, the rumor spread she was a lesbian.

An awkward silence ensued. She and Derek had run out of things to say. *Think, Joya, think. What's a good safe topic? His job. People liked to talk about their jobs.*

"What is it about construction you like?" she asked to ease the tense silence.

Derek thought for a moment. "I like working with my hands and I like it that I don't have to attend meetings. I finish the job I'm given and that's that. Basically I come to work stress-free and I leave that way. My biggest worry is making sure my crew meets the required deadline. It's up to me to turn nothing into something and take an eyesore and turn it into a palace."

"But it must be backbreaking, tiresome work," Joya commented, liking the thought he'd put into his response. Derek was no one's fool.

His brown eyes lit up as he warmed to his subject. "It can be, but when you're done you feel proud of what you've accomplished. Even though you're working within certain confines you're able to bring creativity to a project. It's like an artist putting a personal stamp on a piece. You're leaving a legacy behind."

"And there's something to be said about not having to play the political corporate game. It's one of the reasons I liked being a flight attendant," Joya added. "I showed up for work, flew from point A to B, went home and collected my check. My boss was the senior flight attendant on that crew and if we didn't see eye to eye then I traded the next trip and got a new boss."

"You're speaking in the past tense. Didn't you like the autonomy of being master of your own fate?"

"Yes, but I'm no longer with the airline."

"You quit?" Derek said, putting it into words and making it sound final. "I just can't imagine you not getting along with anyone."

It occurred to Joya that he was being snide.

"There are people that set my teeth on edge," she said, looking directly at him. Let him imagine the worst.

He chuckled softly, apparently finding humor in her words. "I hope I'm not one of them. You've always been civil, even when those two winners your grandma employed were trying to get over on you. You could have been hell on wheels but you weren't."

"You mean Deborah and LaTisha?"

"Yeah. Those two pieces of work."

Joya's cheeks heated up. A compliment from Derek? Backhanded as it was. She was enjoying the back and forth. And much as she hated to admit it, she was enjoying spending time with him.

Derek paused in front of the raised stage used for outdoor performances. A hopeful guitarist strummed a guitar that needed tuning. The case lay at his feet with pitifully few coins in it.

"I have to go," Derek said. "I'm ripe for a shower and there are a couple of things I need to do before tonight's gig. I'll see you a little after seven then?"

"I'll be there."

Derek began a slow jog, heading for his grandmother's house, a stone's throw from the boardwalk. Joya took off in the opposite direction. She was already thinking about what to wear to the Twilight Jam. She'd seen the way Derek looked at Emilie, quite obviously he was interested, and she'd felt a twinge of jealousy. She wanted him to look at her the same way he'd looked at Emilie, and she couldn't fathom why.

At Flamingo Beach General Granny J was being examined by Dr. Benjamin.

"Are you done poking at me?" she groused, "I'm liable to be black and blue all over." She'd had enough of lying in bed trying to digest inedible food. She wanted out.

"All done," the doctor said, patting her upper arm. He was treating her like a child, or even worse, an old lady who needed to be patronized.

She wasn't about to be appeased or dismissed. "Okay. I'm alive, so when can I go home?"

"Didn't I say tomorrow?" Dr. Benjamin flipped through the clipboard he was carrying. "You're doing very well, and you'll do even better if you stick to the recommended diet and get some exercise."

"Tomorrow can't come fast enough," Granny J moaned. "I have a business that I've neglected. Lord knows what I'm going to find when I get back. My granddaughter has been running the shop and although she's efficient enough she's not exactly an entrepreneur."

"Your granddaughter seems quite capable to me. By the way, she's a lovely young woman and she strikes me as smart. Any changes she's made will probably be for the better." Dr. Ben's cheeks were ruddy under his light complexion. He took off his glasses and stuck them in his pocket.

Granny J shot up in bed. "Changes? What changes? What are you not telling me?"

"Take a deep breath now and settle down. Change can be very good. No one wants to remain stagnant."

Granny J flashed her warm welcoming smile, the kind she used on customers. She eyed the doctor slyly. "Some changes aren't good. You've met my Joya. Isn't she a lovely woman?"

"Beautiful, compassionate and smart," Dr. Benjamin said, his face turning an alarming shade of crimson.

Granny J folded her arms across her chest. "If she's all that, then why isn't a young, handsome doctor like you asking her out?"

"I just might," Dr. Benjamin said, patting her hand as if she were a child. "At the very least I'll take it under consideration."

Good lord, the man needed nudging. In her day, men stepped up to the plate and took care of business. She'd have to find a reason to make this happen. The Hamills could definitely use a doctor in the house.

Derek finished putting the final coat of primer on the bathroom wall. He'd gotten back from his run energized and found Nana asleep and Mari wanting to run an errand. All in all, it was the perfect time to get stuff done.

He pressed his nose to the new window and saw the sun slowly disappearing into the sea. He had just enough time to jump into the shower and change before Joya stopped by. He was looking forward to spending this time with her. There was more going on in that pretty head than he'd initially been led to believe.

Twenty minutes later he'd showered, shaved and changed into a pair of khaki shorts and polo shirt. He'd also slipped on a pair of canvas boat shoes and, as an afterthought, had slapped on cologne. Finally he stuck his head into Nana's room to see how she was doing.

She was lying still, hands clasped on her stomach as if she was laid out. A pack of cigarettes remained in easy reach, as were several books of matches.

Derek eased her door closed.

"Nothing wrong with my hearing. You going out, boy?"

Derek tiptoed back into her room. He kissed her cheek. "Yes, can I get you something before I go?"

"Nope, I have everything I need." Nana sat up in bed and reached for a cigarette. She wrinkled her nose. "What's that smell?"

"Cologne."

"Nobody puts on cologne just to hear some guys jam." She sucked what was left of her teeth. "You all dressed up 'cause of some woman."

"You're too smart for me. I'm out of here, Nana."

Derek left her smoking those damn cigarettes and went out on the porch to wait for Joya. By the time she got there maybe he wouldn't have that nasty smoky smell clinging to him.

He hated to admit it, but he was fascinated with Joya and normally he ran from that type. She'd struck him as high-maintenance, more than a little demanding and highstrung. But he liked how dedicated she was to her grandmother and how committed to taking care of her business.

Derek had heard the talk around town about how Joya had tried to change Quen. He'd heard all the speculation about why the marriage had deteriorated. It didn't take long to find out stuff in Flamingo Beach, fabricated or otherwise.

Well hell, his marriage had deteriorated, too, because he'd spent way too much time at work. He'd justified the time spent away as earning the money to buy his wife all the things she wanted. He'd gotten caught up in the corporate game and keeping up with the Joneses. In retrospect he should never have gotten married. There hadn't been much between them to begin with. They'd just mistaken physical attraction for true love. When the bloom wore off the rose they'd tried to make it work and from there everything had begun unraveling.

"Hey, Derek?" Joya had arrived. When she stepped out of her red convertible, everything inside him went still.

She had on pants that stopped a little below the knee

and a shirt showing an inch or so of skin at the middle. For once she wasn't wearing those ridiculous heels. The whole effect was of a tiny, fragile person who needed his help. Derek met her halfway down the walk.

Joya waved an envelope and a set of keys at him. "I've got the deposit. These keys will give you access to the store if I'm not around. Check inside and make sure it's the agreed-to amount."

He took the envelope from her but didn't open it right away. "Want to come in and see what I'm doing to the house before we run off?"

"I'd love to," she answered, surprising him. "I've always admired this house."

He held the front door open for her, and she walked in, stopping to look down, a slow smile curving her mouth.

"Bamboo floors," she said, "Nice."

"Yes. I laid them myself because they're durable and in keeping with a beach house. If Nana decides to put the house up for sale, bamboo floors will increase the value, don't you think?"

Joya was too busy wandering around the great room and inspecting the fireplace that seldom got lit to answer. She ran a hand over the top of the marble mantelpiece. "This is nice."

"My workmanship," Derek acknowledged with some pride. "Can I get you something to drink?"

"No thanks. I'm saving myself for that wine you promised."

"Derek, you have somebody there?" Nana croaked from her bedroom.

"A friend stopped by," Derek shouted back.

"A woman friend. You going to bring her in to meet me?"

Nothing like being put on the spot. "Nana doesn't get out much, do you mind?" Derek whispered.

"Not at all."

Derek took Joya's hand and began leading her through a maze of rooms. "Excuse the mess," he said. "The house is currently under construction. As you can see, I'm working on several rooms."

"Not a problem."

"Derek, you bringing your friend to see me or not?" Nana Belle reminded them.

"We're coming, Nana."

Derek rolled his eyes and they burst out laughing. "She's a character."

"She just might have my grandmother beat," Joya agreed, actually liking that Derek's large hand was wrapped around hers.

Derek paused in front of a door that was slightly ajar. "I might as well warn you, Belle is a heavy smoker, so be prepared."

"I was a flight attendant, remember? I'm used to

people disconnecting the smoke alarm in airplane bathrooms so that they can light up. I'll manage."

Joya was taking it all in stride. He liked that and guessed his eccentric grandmother wouldn't faze her one bit. Pushing the door open he spotted Nana Belle sitting straight up in bed sucking on one of her cancer sticks.

"This is Joya Hamill," Derek said, nudging Joya forward. "She and I are heading out to the beach to hear the people jam."

"You're Trudy and Leland's girl," Belle said, staring at Joya. "You must look just like your mother."

"You knew my parents?"

"Yes, ma'am. Come closer, child, so I can see you."

Joya approached the bed until she was close enough to touch Nana.

Derek was always amazed at Nana's long-term memory and the stories she could recount. Having a visitor had made her alert. It had been a long time since he'd seen her this alive.

"Is my great-grandson courting you?" she asked, peering into Joya's face.

"Uh... We..."

He placed a hand on Joya's forearm. "We need to go or all the good spots are going to be taken. Mari's in her room, Nana, you call her if you need anything."

"I'd rather suffer in silence."

Derek did another eye roll and tugged on Joya's hand. "We need to go."

"Can I leave my car out front or do I need to move it?" Joya asked.

"Your car will be just fine. We'll cut through the sun porch. Did you bring the blanket? Call Mari if you need anything, Nana."

"You two have a good time." She sounded sad, as if unhappy they were leaving.

"It was nice meeting you, Mrs. Carter," Joya said, to the old lady.

"Call me Ms. Belle."

His great-gran lit up another cigarette. She blew a huge smoke ring and closed her eyes. They'd been dismissed.

Outside, Joya said, "Thanks for introducing me to your great-grandmother." Derek had found a flashlight and the promised wine while Joya retrieved an old blanket from the trunk of her car; the kind you kept for emergencies. They were set.

"Nana's an odd duck, but she means well."

"I've heard so much about her from my own grandmother that I feel I know her. She is just as Granny J described her. Direct and feisty."

"You'd have to be to survive five husbands," Derek said, tongue-in-cheek. "She's a tough old bird and doesn't suffer fools easily.

"One husband was enough for me," Joya said under her breath.

"Yeah, I agree. I'd be hard-pressed to walk down an aisle again."

"You were married?" Joya asked. "I had no idea."

"All of five years. So much for happily ever after."

"What happened?"

"A lot of things. Work got in the way. I didn't give her the attention she needed."

"You worked 24/7? Construction gets that busy?"

"I wasn't always in construction," Derek said cryptically.

Joya's gray eyes scanned his face, and he realized he'd gotten her full attention. He'd said too much.

"What did you do before you were in construction?" she asked.

"A bunch of different things."

He didn't have anything to hide or be ashamed of. It was just that he'd put the corporate world behind him. Today he used his engineering skills in a very different way and if Joya was going to hinge her liking or disliking him on his current profession, well, that didn't speak well of her.

He'd had it with superficial people and those needing and wanting to keep up with the Joneses. From his experience the Joneses were usually in a lot of debt. It cost money to keep up appearances.

They'd reached the area where the jam session was held and their conversation was put on hold. Several people had brought folding chairs and there were cars double-parked, some illegally on the boardwalk. Every available speck of sand was covered with a blanket or cloth. The smell of beer and barbecue competed with the scent of brine from the ocean.

Derek held Joya's hand as they picked their way around an amiable Saturday-night crowd.

"We should have gotten here earlier," he groused. "There's no way we're getting close to the stage."

"What about up the beach a bit?" Joya suggested. "We'll be able to hear the tunes even if we can't see the musicians."

"Good idea," Derek said making a U-turn.

They walked up the beach away from where the crowd gathered. It was probably not a good idea to be in a secluded spot with Joya. Parts of his body were already at half-mast.

But maybe tonight was the kind of night to let your other head rule. Tomorrow, when reality returned, he could deal with the consequences.

Chapter 12

The jam session ran over its allotted time, largely because the weather was drizzly. The musicians, concerned about their equipment, refused to play until the rain stopped, and although there was no real downpour, moods were somber.

Joya and Derek found an isolated spot up the beach close to the lighthouse. They figured that if there was a torrential downpour the lighthouse would provide shelter. A few couples having the same idea had spread blankets behind the rocks. And, although they couldn't see their neighbors, the fruity smells of wine, barbecue and citronella candles scented the air, providing evidence of their proximity.

"Excellent choice of wine," Joya said, sipping on her second glass while surreptitiously checking the label. There was just enough light coming from the gas lanterns on the boardwalk to make out the label. It truly was an outstanding zinfandel and must have set Derek back at least a twenty-spot. He was full of surprises, a man of many layers, she decided.

"At one point I kept a cellar," he let slip.

"You did?"

She wasn't sure she believed him.

"The house I owned came with one. Rather than let it go empty I decided I would learn what I could about wine and start collecting."

Joya sat back on her blanket. Her feet were bare and her toenails were painted sugarplum-pink. She curled and uncurled her toes and decided, why not play along with him?

"So what did you do with this house you owned?

"Sold it. Hey, that guy on the sax is pretty good."

He didn't seem to want to discuss his wine collection or his house. But she did.

"I don't think I've heard him before. Maybe he's new to town," she said.

"Everyone's new these days. Flamingo Beach is quite the hot spot. We're the flavor of the month, judging by the houses going up. Mind you, I'm not complaining because it means work for me."

There was a rumble of thunder in the distance, followed by the crash of lightning.

"Uh-oh," Joya said. "That doesn't sound good."

"Don't tell me you're afraid of a little rain?" Derek joked.

"A little I don't mind. A lot—that's a whole other story." She stood and grabbed at the blanket he was still sitting on.

"Okay, Ms. Subtle, I get it." Derek stood before she tried to pull the blanket out from under him. He picked up the wine bottle with a third of its contents left and draped an arm around Joya's shoulders.

"Where to, madam?"

"The lighthouse or we make a run for it down the beach and hope that we make it to my car or your house before it pours. My hair doesn't hold up to rain."

Another crash of thunder made it sound as if the sky were splitting in two. Forks of lightning lit up the surrounding area.

"Bye-bye jam session. No one's stupid enough to risk being electrocuted. It's the lighthouse for us."

Derek swooped her off her feet and began to run toward the tower.

"What are you doing?" she screamed, quite liking his Neanderthal approach, but reluctant to admit it. The wine must have gone to her head, either that or Derek and his offbeat personality had gotten under her skin.

"Where did everyone else go?" Joya asked, realizing they were alone. She wrapped her arms around Derek's neck to anchor herself.

"They all had the good sense to find shelter a long time ago. But not us."

Joya giggled, liking the lighthearted way he poked fun at them.

Exactly one second before the sky exploded and rain pelted down, Derek kicked opened the lighthouse door and set her down inside.

"That was close," he said, removing the flashlight from his pocket and illuminating the interior briefly. "I wonder where everyone else is hiding."

"Right now, the only thing I'm concerned about is not having some creepy-crawly thing run over my foot."

Derek shone the flashlight around, making shadows on the walls, and found steps leading upward. "I'm at your service, princess. I am prepared to do battle with any rodent or palmetto bug we encounter."

Another bolt of thunder had Joya grabbing Derek by the arm and clinging. Outside, angry waves slammed against the pilings and sheets of rain sounded like a giant crumpling cellophane.

"Doesn't appear that it's about to let up anytime soon," he commented.

"Then we might as well either explore or get comfortable."

"How about we do both? It's rumored this place is haunted, I say we go find the ghost."

Something about having Derek nearby was very comforting, and made her ready to take on any ghost. She had the feeling he was the type of guy who took good care of his ladies. Too bad she wasn't one of them.

Where did that come from?

Joya still had a hold of his arm. Up close and personal she couldn't miss the delicious smell coming from him. Maybe it was a good idea to explore and not get comfortable. Who knew what she might do? No, *they* might do. They couldn't be trusted together.

"I'm leading the way," Derek said shining the flashlight in front of them and lighting a path.

Joya followed him toward the narrow stone steps that no two people could possibly mount side by side. She kept a fistful of his shirt in her hand as they continued to climb.

For some strange reason she was getting really spooked. Maybe it was the darkness, or it might have something to do with Derek bringing up the story that the lighthouse was haunted. Then again, maybe it had to do with the realization that the two of them were here alone, and no one had seen them enter. If anything happened, no one would know.

They'd reached the top. Through a window she could see an angry sky lit up by lightning and she could hear the ocean's roar below.

Something furry brushed against her foot. Joya's scream pierced the darkness. She leapt into the air, bringing Derek with her.

"What's wrong? What happened?" His voice was close to her ear.

Her breathing now came in quick little bursts. She was close to hyperventilating. "A mouse. A rat," she said when she could bring herself to speak. "Something with fur and claws. It was disgusting."

Derek, despite her death grip on him, shone the flashlight around the open space. Whatever it was had gone into hiding.

"I want to go home," Joya pleaded, looking uneasily around and expecting whatever it was to reappear.

"You'd rather brave a storm than deal with a mouse that's more scared of you than you of it?"

"That's right. I hate creepy-crawlies, and I hate mice."

Derek hugged her to him. "I'm here to protect you, girl." The flashlight wobbled in his hand.

For a brief second, Joya allowed herself to relax and trust him. She let Derek fold her into his arms. They kissed again, and her arms wrapped around his neck and she gave in to the passion, the feeling of being swept away. Another quick brush of their lips, and again that instant combustion, the feeling her body was on fire.

Derek's hands were warm on her bare stomach. He began a sensual massage, a supple kneading of flesh. Those same hands found their way to her breasts. Derek's rough palms created a friction that caused her nipples to pebble and harden. His fingers slipped under the demi-cups of her bra, tweaking her nipples and setting off another round of heat. Every nerve was wired.

She was alive, pulsing and suffused with heat. Her loins felt heavy and her body close to exploding. She bit the side of Derek's neck and pressed herself against him, fitting her lithe body against his solid one. He was rock-hard and throbbing. Joya ran a hand over his butt and gave a little squeeze. Then things went rapidly out of control.

Joya's shirt was pulled over her head, and she did nothing to stop him. Simultaneously, she unzipped his pants and reached inside to release him. Then, holding him in one hand, she used her saliva to dampen a finger and draw circles around the rim of his erect penis.

Derek's groan told her she'd hit a sweet spot. He brought her up hard against him and the flashlight rolled across the floor, causing them to jump.

"Stop me now if you don't want this to go any further," he said, on a ragged breath.

Joya didn't want to stop him. She was living in the moment with no expectations beyond this. Derek was making her feel like a woman again, and from the sounds of his uneven breathing, she hadn't forgotten what it took to make a man happy. Still, if he hadn't brought protection with him, things would come to a grinding halt. Now that would be disappointing.

"Joya?"

"I'm here, baby."

"I need to get a condom from my wallet."

Hallelujah! He'd come prepared. That also indicated responsibility.

Derek kicked off his pants then bent to retrieve his wallet from his back pocket. Joya removed what was left of her clothes. When Derek straightened he handed her the condom. "Come on, baby, help me slip this on."

She used her hands and mouth to do so as Derek braced himself against the wall. His eyes were closed, his breathing strained. Rodents were forgotten. Joya stood on tiptoes to wrap her arms around his neck. Derek's hands clamped around her buttocks and slowly lifted her until she was impaled. He began a slow sensuous thrust. With every entry, his thrusts grew in intensity as she jiggled and bounced against him, feeling as if she would burst out of her skin.

Derek nibbled on a nipple and Joya threw her head back. Her whole body ignited with the heat that seared through her. She was throbbing in places she didn't think were possible. Then Derek's whole body convulsed and with a final thrust he exploded. She bit down on his shoulder, let go and hurtled over the top.

Seconds turned to minutes and Derek still held onto her. Eventually he planted a kiss on her lips before setting her down. Then he retrieved the flashlight that had rolled into the corner, found his pants and climbed into them. Joya gathered her clothing and quickly got dressed. Without saying a word she followed him down the staircase and into the night.

Outside, the wind was still howling, but the rain had turned to drizzle. Only the occasional drenched stray dog roamed the boardwalk and there was no evidence of the aborted jam session.

Derek appeared lost in thought, and conversation was kept at a bare minimum. They walked back to Belle's, where Joya had left her car. Awkward as this was turning out to be, she had no regrets. She'd done what felt right and had been a willing participant in their lovemaking. She'd come to it with no expectations beyond what had happened tonight. She only hoped Derek was of the same mind, since he hadn't even tried holding her hand again.

When she reached her car, Derek gave her a peck on the cheek, the kind a brother gives a sister.

"Are you okay to drive?" he asked.

"I'm fine. The wine's pretty much worn off. Thanks for spending your evening with me."

"I've enjoyed every last second of it." His finger grazed her cheek. "Drive safely now. See you Monday."

Joya climbed into her vehicle and Derek shut the door. She waved at him and started up the car. It wasn't until she was halfway across town that the full impact of what she'd done hit her. She'd made love to a man she barely knew. Worse than that, technically he was her employee and also one of her customers.

Enjoyable as it was, it just couldn't happen again. She wouldn't let it!

"I want to see what you did with my store," Granny J insisted as Joya hung a left on Blue Heron.

"How about tomorrow, Gran? Today you really should stay in bed."

She made another left on Bird Road and a right on Ibis. They were now only a few minutes from Flamingo Row.

Since Granny J had been released from the hospital she hadn't stopped carping. She was in one of her stubborn moods.

Joya had picked her grandmother up in the Lincoln Continental figuring it would be a more comfortable ride, but granny hadn't wanted to get comfortable. The store was all that she talked about and there was no changing the conversation.

After she'd parked the Lincoln in the back of the house, Joya tried once again.

"Tomorrow will be time enough, Gran," she said, helping the old lady out of the back seat. Her bags could wait until after she'd gotten her settled. "Dr. Benjamin said you needed to be off your feet for at least a few more days. He wants you to take things slow."

"It's my store and I want to see it," the old lady insisted, jerking her elbow out of Joya's hold. "I'll rest far better if I see what changes you've made."

Instead of starting up the path to the house, Granny toddled across the scrap of back lawn and toward the front where the store was. Joya reluctantly followed her. It was impossible to talk Granny J out of anything after she'd made up her mind.

The old lady stood on the sidewalk staring at the Craftsman-style cottage that served double duty as both her home and her store. Her lips were pursed and she jiggled her foot.

"What's with the window boxes? What's with the geraniums and impatiens?"

"Don't they look pretty?" Joya said, trying to appease her. "It makes Joya's Quilts look festive and homey."

"It looks like a little old lady's house."

Granny took a few hesitant steps up the walkway then mounted the three little steps leading to the porch.

"I don't remember buying a wicker settee," she muttered.

"You didn't. Chet and Harley were going to throw it out in the trash. It seemed perfectly good to me so I asked if I could have it. Doesn't it look pretty painted that nice rose color? It's a good place to display quilts and they're bound to catch the eyes of passersby. Did I tell you how well our sale did?"

"We've never had a sale. Didn't need one."

Granny J was breathing raggedly now. Climbing the few steps and her fussing had taken its toll. She leaned against a post on the verandah and looked out onto the still-quiet Flamingo Row. It was Sunday morning and most everyone was at church. They should have been, too, except Joya thought the old lady wasn't ready for the long church service and the lengthy socializing afterward. She'd been right, Granny needed to rest.

"What are those iron things sticking up out of the ground over there?" Granny J asked. "A body's liable to trip and hurt themselves. Since it's my sidewalk we'll probably get sued."

Joya looked in the direction her grandmother was pointing. She'd asked the same question earlier that week.

"Those will eventually be flamingos, Gran. They're being created in honor of the centennial. The city commissioned a sculptor from up north to make one hundred flamingos. They're to be strategically placed through the town and citizens are invited to dress them. They'll go up for auction shortly."

Granny J snorted. "What nonsense."

"Not nonsense, they're potential money-makers for the Beach. There'll be a prize for the best-dressed bird. There's a lot of press associated with those birds. I'm thinking I could talk the city and the creator into putting one on our front lawn."

Granny looked horrified. A hand clapped over her mouth. "Whatever for?"

"That flamingo will bring us business and we need money, Gran."

She snorted again. "I can't imagine who would want to spend money on a tarted-up flamingo?"

"Plenty of people. Some cities got big money for the pigs and cows they auctioned, so why not Flamingo Beach? I'm exhausted."

Joya flopped onto the wicker two-seater hoping

Gran would get the message and join her. But no, Granny J remained standing, a hand on the railing, trying her best not to huff and puff.

"Fine, we can have a pink flamingo on the front lawn if you think it would help business," she said eventually. "But it's got to wear a quilted dress and a sun bonnet that I make."

"You got it, Gran." Even though she was clearly tired, Granny's enthusiasm was slowly returning. The senior citizen had gone through quite a bit these last few weeks. "You can design the outfit yourself and make it. Maybe we'll even win the prize."

"We'll win. Just wait until you see what I have in mind."

This was more like the old Gran she was used to, positive, obstinate and determined. Joya wondered what her reaction would be when she saw the store's interior and what a difference the repositioning of furniture made. And that was the tip of the iceberg—when construction began tomorrow, Gran would really start yelping.

Thoughts of change brought to mind Derek. Joya's cheeks grew heated at the thought of the unbridled passion they'd shared, their lack of inhibition and the fact that they'd been so in sync with each other's needs.

Gran took her keys out of the ancient white leather

purse she carried and struggled with the front door. Joya went to help her.

"Don't treat me like an invalid," she said. "I'm perfectly capable of opening up my own store. I've been doing it for years."

Clamping her lips shut, Joya backed off.

Chapter 13

Harley Mancini stepped out of his illegally parked vehicle and onto the cobblestoned road.

"Welcome home, Mrs. Hamill," he called. "Hi Joya. Glad to see you back. Did you get our flowers, Mrs. Hamill?"

"Yes, I did, thank you. I'll be sending you a note." Gran finally got the door opened and preceded Joya inside.

"Oh, my God, what happened here?" she said, clutching her heart.

Joya who was right behind her, and who had been

anticipating a reaction, placed an arm around Granny J's waist.

"Gran, I've organized a few things and moved some furniture so the merchandise shows to its best advantage."

"You call this organized? This isn't the store I remember. It's a mess." The old lady whirled around, clutching her heart again. Joya tightened her hand around Gran's waist.

As she stepped inside the store, Joya realized why her grandmother had reacted in such an outraged manner. The place *was* a mess. Quilts had been swept off the shelves and lay in tangles on the floor. The walls were defaced by ugly graffiti and some of the furniture was broken. Even one of the sewing machines was smashed.

Joya gulped in a deep breath. She needed to stay calm. Her first priority was to get Granny seated—and fast. She spotted an old armchair still intact and led the shocked old lady over.

"I'll get you a glass of water, Gran, and then I'm calling the police."

"Police?" Gran repeated still in shock. "Why would we need the police?"

"Because we've been broken into. That window wasn't open when I left."

"I'll call the police, you tend to your grandmother," a deep male voice said from behind them.

Joya turned to see Derek standing at the entrance of the store surveying the destruction.

"What are you doing here?" she asked.

"Get your grandmother water, and I'll answer the question."

Yes, yes, Gran should be her first priority. Joya hurried into the back room, not sure what state that would be in.

That room was in the same disastrous condition. It looked like a whirlwind had hit it. Someone had swept everything off the shelves and torn out the pages of Gran's ledgers. Paperwork and ripped-up receipts were strewn all over the wooden floors. Joya found a glass, picked her way around the debris, and found the water cooler. She filled up the glass and hurried back.

Derek was on the phone talking to the police when Joya handed her grandmother the water.

"Take slow sips," she instructed.

Granny J just held onto the glass staring vacantly out at the room.

"You need to get over here on the double," Joya overheard Derek say to the police. "Yeah, it looks like there was a break-in. No, no one's hurt."

After Derek hung up he stepped over the destruction on the floor and came toward them.

"Mrs. Hamill, why don't you go to bed? Joya and I will take it from here."

"I'm not an invalid," Granny J said, bristling, but she didn't protest when Joya took both of her hands and helped her out of the chair.

"Take a nap for a couple of hours, Gran, while we deal with the cops and file a report."

Joya helped her grandmother around the debris and toward the door leading to the private entrance. It took her almost half an hour to get Granny J settled because, emotionally exhausted as the old lady was, she just couldn't fall asleep. Joya had to trick her into taking a sleeping pill.

When she returned to the store, a patrol car with Lionel and Greg was already there, and a small crowd had gathered on the verandah talking. Among them were Peter and Dustin Millard, owners of the Vintage Place next door and Chet and Harley from the flower shop.

Derek was still standing in the middle of the store where she'd left him, tight-lipped and wired.

"How are you holding up?" he asked, placing an arm around Joya's shoulders and hugging her close.

Tears stung the back of Joya's lids as she pressed her face into his shirt. Her heart hurt, but she still registered his familiar scent and welcomed his comfort.

Derek smelled clean and felt safe. Right now he was the only support she had.

"I've been better," Joya sniffed. "Gran sure as heck didn't need to come home to this."

"I'll handle the officers if you'd like," Derek offered. "I'd hoped to speak with you about sprucing up the store's exterior, that's why I came by, but that will have to wait."

"I thought we were going to renovate the interior only?" Joya said, distracted, although at that moment she had more than renovations on her mind.

"We talked briefly about keeping all the stores' exteriors the same, just adding a few unique touches to define what they're about. For example, the bright colors and artistic signage tells you All About Flowers is a flower shop."

It was an interesting concept, but right now there were other things on her mind, like this latest act of vandalism. Someone must have it in for Joya and her grandmother.

Derek, hearing the cop cars pull up out front, met the officers on the verandah and escorted them inside. Greg and Lionel stood taking in the mess.

"How come your alarm didn't go off?" Lionel asked. "We'll need the names of everyone who has keys or knows the security code." He had a pad out.

"I have keys and so does my grandmother. Portia,

our part-time employee has keys. And I've given keys to Shore Construction because they're starting work tomorrow. The alarm wasn't on."

Derek spoke up, "Shore Construction would be me and I assure you I had nothing to do with this."

"That window was open when I came in." She pointed to the open window and the chiffon curtain fluttering in the breeze.

Greg Santana navigated his way around the tossed items and came toward her. "First things first. We get a detective over to dust for fingerprints." He was already speaking into a radio summoning help.

"Whoever it was came through that window rather than the front door, you think?" Lionel asked, stating the obvious. "Please don't touch anything until the detective gets here."

Despite Joya's determination to stay strong, her eyes brimmed over with tears. Derek handed her a handkerchief from his back pocket, and she blew her nose loudly. She wanted to be strong, but it just wasn't happening.

Two hours later, after being grilled by a detective and having had the store dusted for fingerprints, Joya went off to check on Granny J. Finding the old lady sleeping, she returned to the store. Derek was still there trying to put things back together.

Side by side they worked, reassembling furniture

and putting items in the trash and through it all, the chemistry between them was palpable. If Derek glanced over at her it was as if she'd been zapped by a lightning bolt. Just having him here was a big help and it wasn't only because he provided muscle.

How could she ever hope to pay him back? Derek would be insulted if she offered him money. Maybe…it was just an idea. Maybe she could ask him to escort her to the wedding. He could probably use an evening out.

She waited until they'd cleaned up almost everything before posing the question.

"What are you doing next Saturday evening?" Joya asked.

Derek folded a quilt with a Log Cabin pattern and placed it on a shelf. "Next Saturday is a long ways away. What did you have in mind?"

"How would you like to go with me to a wedding?"

"Quen and Chere's wedding?"

He made it sound like he knew them.

"Yes, that's the one."

"Let me think about it," Derek said.

And instead of leaving it alone she countered. "What's there to think about?"

"I was invited but said no."

Joya's mouth opened and shut. She was surprised that Derek even knew the bride and groom.

"I'm sorry I asked, since obviously you'd already made up your mind you weren't going."

There was a twinkle in his brown eyes when he said, "I could be persuaded to change my mind. I didn't fancy going solo."

She brightened considerably and flirted right back. "Good. If your arm can be twisted and since I told them I'd go, would you consider being my guest?"

Derek touched the tip of a finger to his lips. "I might be persuaded to be your date in exchange for a kiss."

"Okay." She came toward him, got on tiptoe and brushed her lips against his. "There."

Derek whipped a proprietary arm around her. "You can do better than that."

His tongue was in her mouth before she knew it, and she was enjoying his passion-filled kiss. Their tongues dipped and danced, melded and collided. Derek made love to her mouth just as he'd done to her body with an expertise and tenderness she'd never experienced before.

A throat cleared behind them. "Uh, excuse me. Joya, we'll need your signature on this report."

Lionel held out the police report she'd filled out earlier. She scanned it quickly and, convinced everything was in order, signed it and handed it back to Lionel.

After Lionel left them she returned to the earlier

conversation, "You never did give me an answer," she said to Derek.

"Okay I'll go. But only because you asked."

There was nothing left to do now but lock up the store. And this time she was definitely putting on the alarm. She again thanked Derek for his help and went off to check on Gran.

One week later, construction at Joya's Quilts was underway. Joya and Derek were now butting heads about the opposing visions each had for the store. At times Granny J was barely speaking to them. She walked around in her bedroom slippers huffing, snorting and nixing every suggestion as "plain wrong."

Derek wanted to do things one way. Joya another. But eventually Joya did come around to Derek's way of thinking because, much as she hated to admit it, Derek's way made better sense. His suggestions were ultimately more pleasing to the eye, more practical and less expensive.

The police were still stumped by the break-in. You'd think in a town the size of Flamingo Beach someone had to have seen something. But so far, no leads. What the police had done was increase surveillance, and both the *Flamingo Beach Chronicle* and the *Southern Tribune* had published articles about the break-in. Now all of the store owners were being extra careful about locking up and setting their alarms.

While the store was being renovated, business was being conducted from the porch. Joya had finally convinced Granny J that anything that had sat in the store for over six months needed to be on sale.

"It's a good time to unload stuff that's not selling," Joya wheedled. "Call up the people whose things you took on consignment and let them know what we're doing. If they're not happy with it, then have them take their quilts back."

After a great deal of discussion, Granny J had reluctantly conceded that sales were a good idea. She saw how much business and enthusiasm they generated and so stopped giving Joya flack. And, during this time of renovation, the quilt guild held their meetings at Eileen Brown's.

The women had loved Joya's idea of making commemorative quilts, and every single person had gone to work. Those without day jobs were making quilts like crazy and practically working around the clock. Eileen had made another quilt for Molly Williams to replace the one that had been damaged, and although Joya had lost her shirt on it, Molly was pleased with the new quilt and that was what mattered.

Meanwhile Portia, the part-time worker was a big help. She showed up on time and did whatever Joya asked her to do. Granny J was still in recuperation mode and spending minimal time on the premises. At times it was just Joya and Portia working from a porch that didn't have air conditioning. But items were moving and that was what mattered.

One afternoon when there was a lull in sales, Joya and Portia sat on the verandah enjoying a cool glass of lemonade. On the Row, workmen were positioning the flamingos in optimum spots. A man who looked to be the artist was supervising them.

"Hey," Joya called to him. "I wouldn't mind having one of those birds on my property."

He was fiftyish with a long graying braid.

"I'll have to clear it with the city," he called back. "One would look real nice on your front porch don't you think?"

"All About Flowers right next door is owned by the mayor's son. We could erect the flamingo on our joint property line." Joya made a private note to talk to Harley and have him talk to Chet about the idea.

She turned to Portia. "When does school end?"

"In a couple of weeks. I'm trying to decide whether to go on for a BA or not. If that happens I can't continue to work in the shop."

"Why?"

"Because I'd be leaving town."

"You wouldn't consider going to Pelican Island

U?" Joya asked, her brain already calculating what she would do about getting Granny J reliable help.

"I asked LaTisha what she thought about that idea…"

"LaTisha? You're in touch with her?" Joya hadn't thought the two were friends. They were different as night and day.

"Yeah, every now and then I see her. She misses working at the shop."

"That's a surprise."

The phone rang and the conversation was tabled. Joya braved the sawdust and paint fumes and went inside to answer. Sticking a finger in one ear, she tried her best to tune out the sounds of hammering. She was keenly aware of Derek's presence and could feel his eyes on her, but kept her mission in mind. She made it to the phone seconds before the answering machine picked up and made a note to purchase another cordless.

"Joya's Quilts."

"Hey, it's Emilie. Why are you shouting?"

"We're under construction, remember?"

"So you are," Emilie said. "I tried your cell but you didn't answer. I may have found the perfect job for you. It's not quite what you were looking for, but it's got possibilities. It's yours if you want it. I've already put in a good word for you."

Emilie explained that the banquet manager at the Flamingo Beach Spa and Resort needed an assistant. This person would help book events and act as a liaison with decorators and caterers. The pay wasn't huge, but the position might lead to other things.

It figured an offer like this would pop up when Granny still wasn't up to running her shop. Tempting as it was, Joya didn't plan on abandoning her, not until she was a hundred percent recovered and the renovations were finished. And even then Granny would need help. She needed someone to help keep the books.

Timing was everything. And this timing was bad.

Chapter 14

"Okay, Morris, break's over. We've got windows to install and they've got to get done today."

"Yes, boss."

The worker peeled himself off the floor where he was sitting playing solitaire, and returned to the job that he'd been in the middle of before giving himself a break.

Derek had a tight deadline to meet. He needed to get the renovations at Joya's Quilts completed. For his own reasons he was reluctant to hand the project over. And he was pushing the crew like crazy to finish up. Quills had already been completed and the work at All About Flowers was almost done. A few of the crew were putting the finishing touches on the Vintage Place. But Derek was predicting the quilt shop would turn out to be the nicest of them all.

Shore Construction had won the bid to build those waterfront villas at the Flamingo Beach Resort. Every possible worker and then some would be needed on the job and Preston was already considering hiring more people. He was dangling a huge bonus under Derek's nose to get Joya's completed in the next week or so. That bonus would be used to finish up Nana's house.

There was another reason Derek wanted Joya's Quilts done. Granny J needed to feel needed. Having workers underfoot and the general disorder were taking their toll. She was calling on Joya more and more for every little thing, and Joya was beginning to look worn.

She'd banned the old lady from entering the store because she was worried that the sawdust and paint fumes would hinder her recuperation. Of course, keeping Granny J out of the store was nearly impossible. She'd kicked up a fuss and demanded more attention. Joya spent most of her time running back and forth between the shop and Granny J's house. She had little time for anything else, including him.

That was all going to change tonight. He would

make sure of that. Derek planned on knocking off early, getting home, getting some shuteye and then taking a long shower. He would make one of his more reliable men crew boss and leave him explicit instructions. Tonight at Chere and Quen's wedding, it was going to be all about Joya and Derek.

He'd realized why the attraction was so strong—in so many ways they were similar. Both were devoted to elderly relatives and both really cared about the town. They liked the same foods and music, laughed at the same jokes and in bed they really got along. When Joya let loose she was lots of fun. Belle liked her and Nana Belle did not like everyone, so that counted for something.

Derek put his hard hat back on and focused on the ceiling he was raising with the help of two of the crew. Once that roof was raised they were going to add a loft that would overlook the main floor. It would be used for storage and as a place to display quilts. He worked like a demon for the next couple of hours before throwing in the towel.

"Be sure to clean up and lock up when you leave," he said to the men and began gathering his tools.

"I'll take care of everything, don't you worry, suh," the guy he'd promoted to crew boss said.

Assured that work would continue in his absence, he left them.

Derek had an hour to get himself together and pick Joya up. He'd considered renting a car and then decided against it. This wasn't about making a big impression. If she didn't care to arrive at a wedding in a truck then she won't like his lifestyle anyway. He supposed he could ask her to drive that sporty red Beemer of hers. But why? He had no one to impress.

Nana Belle with her acute hearing heard him the moment he put his key in the lock.

"You're home early, boy," she called from the back room. "Everything okay?"

"Yes, ma'am. I'm going to that wedding I told you about."

"You taking that girl?"

Derek entered his own room before shouting back, "What girl?" He knew that would get her going.

"That pretty granddaughter of Mrs. Hamill's."

"Yeah, I'm taking Joya."

Derek shut his bedroom door and began peeling off clothes. He didn't have much time left to shower and dress and he still had to go get Joya.

After a quick shower, he pulled out one of his old designer business suits from the back of his closet. It had set him back several hundred bucks but fell just the way he liked it.

Mari had been nice enough to iron the light-blue shirt and gray-and-blue striped tie that matched.

She'd also polished his black wingtip shoes. All he had to do was find underwear and socks and begin the business of dressing.

When Derek was done, he brushed his tightly cropped hair and slapped on his favorite cologne.

He was ready to go. He decided to check on Nana Belle before leaving. When he entered the old lady's room, she and Mari were arguing. Mari was, as usual, trying to get Nana to eat and taking quite a bit of guff from the old lady.

"You are one fine young man," Mari said looking up from spooning broth into his great-grandmother's mouth. "Those women are going to be all over you."

"What women?" Derek said brushing fluff off his sleeve. "I'm taking a date."

"Never stopped a woman that I know of," Mari muttered knowingly.

"You be nice to that girl, hear?" Nana admonished. "You hold out her chair for her and get her a drink. And you take pictures, lots of them. I want everyone to tell me how nice the two of you looked."

"Yes, ma'am."

Derek didn't have a clue what he was going to do about pictures. He couldn't just stick a camera in one of his pockets or it would ruin the lines of his suit. He'd have to figure out something to appease

Belle, maybe bribe the photographer or something and have him mail photos to him.

"Come here and let me straighten your tie," Nana said, curving a gnarled finger at him.

Derek sat on her bed and allowed her to fumble with the knot at his throat. Belle's arthritic hands did the best that she could and Derek finished up. Derek kissed her cheek.

"You are the best great-gran that a man could ever have. I love you, Nana."

Tears pooled in Belle's eyes though she struggled to hold them back. She sounded nasal when she said, "Go on, boy. Get! Go enjoy yourself. If that young lady don't realize how lucky she is to have you, then phooey on her."

Derek wasn't about to correct his grandmother and tell her that he and Joya weren't what she in her day would have called courting. Belle would never understand what a hook-up was, and that he was really taking Joya to the wedding because she'd asked him to.

Outside he slapped his hand on the surface of the shiny pickup truck before bounding into the driver's seat. He'd had it hand-waxed earlier and it had cost him plenty. His baby was prettier than any luxury automobile, and a heck of a lot more functional.

Since there wasn't much traffic it took him ten

minutes to go across town, which wasn't bad. Most businesses closed early on Saturday anyway and people took to the beach or headed for backyard barbecues. What else was there to do in a sleepy town like Flamingo Beach, although that was slowly changing? Derek wondered if they'd turn into another Pelican Island with its abundance of jazz clubs and huge African-American library hosting cultural events.

At Flamingo Place Derek pulled up at the guard house and told the guard whom he was there for. His license plate was written down and he was instructed to park in a visitor's spot. His intent was to go right up to Joya's front door as he'd been brought up to do. None of this nonsense about honking a horn out front and waiting for your date to come out.

There was more security at the front desk, this time a woman he vaguely recognized. She gave him a speculative look when he told her he was there for Joya Hamill as if he couldn't possibly be. Then she picked up the phone.

"Ms. Hamill says you're to take a seat and wait. She's on her way down."

That took care of that. He was to be left cooling his heels in the lobby until Joya showed up.

More annoyed than he was willing to admit, Derek sank onto one of the comfortable sofas. He stretched his legs out and checked his shoes for scuff marks. As the seconds ticked by, he loosened the knot of his tie.

Five minutes and then ten went by. They were going to be late if Joya didn't hurry. The elevator door opened and she was there looking cool, beautiful and very collected. This was a different Joya than he was used to. He'd never seen her so done up before.

Her hair had been swept back from her face and pinned up with shiny clips that sparkled. The severity of the style made her gray eyes look huge. She wore makeup, lots of it, and the earrings that hung to her shoulders jingled when she approached. Derek tried not to gape.

Joya's bare bronzed shoulders were exposed and the turquoise dress clung to every curve and then some. Derek's glance slid to her shapely legs, slyly scoping her out from her sexy sandals and painted toes to her tight calves that bunched as she walked. He'd like nothing better than to take her back to bed and hear those little mewling noises she made when he touched her in a sensitive spot.

Not now—they had a wedding to attend. Maybe if he got lucky later. Right now he needed to remember his manners and find his tongue.

"You look lovely," he said, taking Joya's hand and bringing it slowly to his lips.

"You mean I've passed inspection?" If it was meant as a jab it went right over his head. He was too busy taking in the package.

"More than passed inspection. You're going to drive every man in that church crazy."

Joya tapped his arm playfully with her purse. "Just look at you with your fine self. The women are going to be wanting me dead."

"I doubt that. We'll miss the ceremony if we don't hurry. I'll bring my vehicle around."

He considered for just a fraction of a second asking her to take her BMW, and then headed for his truck. How would she handle what he was driving? Would she kick up a fuss?

"I'll walk with you," Joya said, taking his arm.

The female security guard stared at them admiringly. Derek winked at the woman who quickly returned to the magazine she was reading.

By running every amber light, they made it to the Flamingo Beach Baptist Church before the wedding started. The church was filled with guests and those there to gawk. Every pew overflowed with people.

"There might be space next to Tre Monroe," Derek whispered in Joya's ear. "Do you know him? Why is a newlywed attending a wedding alone?"

"Because his wife Jen is the matron of honor," Joya whispered back, as arm-in-arm they started up the aisle.

Derek felt every eye on them but maintained his cool, nodding and smiling at those people who were staring. Joya kept her head high and continued on her way. He'd heard that she didn't have many friends in town, and thought it was brave of her to come, given the circumstances. Most would have turned down an invitation to see an ex-husband married.

Tre motioned to the space next to him and slid over. He and Derek were nodding acquaintances. Derek enjoyed the deejay's radio program and admired him for addressing controversial issues that most stayed away from.

As they squeezed into the space, the *Wedding March* started. People craned their necks to watch the bridal party, led by Jen St. George, come up the aisle. Flash bulbs went off. This could not be easy for Joya, Derek realized. He squeezed her hand and she squeezed back.

Joya hadn't thought it would be this difficult watching her ex-husband wait at the altar to marry another woman. She was no longer in love with Quen, but it didn't make it any easier. Just being in the same church where she'd gotten married was making old memories come alive.

It had taken her back to a time in her life where she'd been self-focused and insistent on having everything just right, from the decorated pews draped in white orchids, to the dancing champagne fountain that played music at the reception. She'd been such a child bride, uncompromising and selfish.

She made herself focus and blanked her expression. Fifty percent of the people here had come to see Chere Adams get married. The other fifty percent were there to watch Joya's reaction. Well, she wouldn't give the busybodies the satisfaction of seeing her lose it.

Granny J had cautioned her right before leaving. "You smile and hold up your head, girl. Hamills are survivors. We're tough as they come."

She wasn't about to let Granny J down. So, somehow she found the strength to smile as the bridesmaids marched up the aisle in form-fitting satin gowns, every color of the rainbow, accompanied by escorts in stylish tuxedos that matched. Parasols of contrasting colors twirled above the women's heads.

Chere, bringing up the rear, looked beautiful in her ankle-length white dress decorated with sequins and ostrich feathers. Even the bouquet made up of white roses and ostrich feathers was typically her. To some it might seem outlandish, but it was definitely Chere. And Quen, the proud groom, was smiling from ear to ear. Joya had never seen him this happy.

Derek squeezed her hand again. She was glad that

he'd come with her. He was being supportive and seemed to understand what she was going through.

Although most of it was a blur, Joya made it through the wedding. She vaguely remembered the choir singing and the old pastor droning on about mutual respect and the ability to compromise. Finally he pronounced the couple husband and wife. And somehow she managed to remain dry-eyed.

"Yeah, we did it!" Chere screamed, kissing her husband every two seconds as she boogied down the aisle. And boogie she did, as only Chere could do, ostrich feathers fluttering.

The cocktail hour followed—an outdoor candle-light event. The Flamingo Beach Spa and Resort had followed the bride's instructions to the letter.

"Emilie's supposed to be here," Joya said, looking around for her friend.

"Isn't that her over there?" Derek pointed to a corner of the patio where a small group of people had gathered.

Yep, there was Emilie in the middle of them. She stood next to a white man Joya didn't know, smiling and tilting her head up to hear what he was saying.

"Who are those people?" she asked Derek.

"The white guy, Rowan James, is a developer. I don't know the others."

Joya caught Emilie's eye. Her friend broke away from the group and rushed toward her, garnering the attention of several men. In her emerald-green dress with the sparkling silver stones and plunging neckline, she stood out like a beacon and her high heels had her towering over most of the guests.

"Your girlfriend's one stylish white woman," Derek said, giving a low whistle.

"Emilie's not white. She's a light-skinned Black woman who doesn't even try to pass."

"Well she had me fooled."

"You wouldn't be the first. Emilie gets to hear some interesting comments and all those awful Negro jokes."

"What are you two grinning at?" Emilie interrupted, her manicured fingers curled around a glass of champagne.

"You. I was just telling Derek that you are frequently mistaken for white."

"Oh that!" She made a face. "Hi Derek, remember me? Emilie Woodward?"

"Great dress," he said, cradling Emilie's hand in his and smiling at her as if she was the wedding cake.

Emilie twirled on her crystal-clear stilettos. "Isn't it, though? And worth every dollar that I paid. Come let me introduce you to my date. He's a developer and fairly new to town. He's putting up those townhouses on the south side. The Resort has been talking to him about the undeveloped land on the other side of the golf course."

Derek twined his fingers through Joya's and began following Emilie. Emilie was sure to quiz Joya about her relationship with Derek later, and that was okay because Joya intended to ask Emilie what was she doing out with Rowan as soon as she got the chance.

Chapter 15

Cocktails over with, the wedding guests moved indoors to a banquet room. A dividing wall separated dining from dancing and a rhythm-and-blues band was tuning up on the other side. Joya looked up at the gigantic lit chandelier and the sconces on the walls and thought it all a bit too ornate for her taste. She wished they'd stayed outside.

"We should go find out where we're sitting," she said, ignoring the looks she was getting as she and Derek walked hand-in-hand.

"You're sitting with us," Emilie said firmly, waving a fistful of place cards she'd picked up from somewhere and leading the way to the lace-covered tables. The centerpieces were bride and bridegroom bears dressed in top hats and veils. The cuddly couples held clusters of helium balloons in their paws.

Waiters and waitresses were carrying huge trays of ribs, pork chops and steak. And off to the side, serving tables held bowls of salads, candied yams, collard greens and peas. There were hams, lobsters, chicken, various kinds of fish and just about any food imaginable. And that was before dessert.

Emilie must have manipulated the seating arrangements so that Emilie and Rowan and Tre and Jen, who'd successfully gotten out of sitting with the wedding party, sat across from Derek and Joya. At the far end were two women no one knew. Joya guessed them to be relatives of Chere's because they bore quite a strong resemblance to her.

As a barbershop quartet roamed, guests dined to the a cappella tunes. Champagne flowed and speeches were endless. Overall, a festive, happy crowd came to celebrate with the bride and groom.

Ian Pendergrass, the owner of the *Flamingo Beach Chronicle* was now toasting the couple. It had been rumored that he and Chere had once had something going, and that he gave her the job at the *Chronicle*. Chere had become an up-and-coming real-estate agent but still held onto her old job.

Playing to the crowd, Ian held his champagne glass up to the light and began his speech.

"It's indeed a pleasure to be here to celebrate the nuptials of Quentin Abraham and Chere Adams. Doesn't the new Mrs. Abraham make a beautiful bride?" Applause broke out at his statement. "She is as lovely on the inside as she is on the outside. The groom is a very lucky man. Isn't that right, gentlemen?"

Another round of applause followed, this time coming primarily from the men.

Chere placed an arm around her husband and laid a big one on him. Mouths must be running fast and furiously. While the people of Flamingo Beach might have come to celebrate with Chere and Quen, they weren't above talking about them. After all, heavyset Chere had snatched up one of the Beach's most eligible bachelors and good men were scarce.

Dinner out of the way, a three-tiered wedding cake complete with sparklers was wheeled in and served. The divider was opened up and the lead singer of the band belted a Barry White tune inviting everyone to join the bride and groom in their first dance. Then began some serious grinding.

"Want to join them?" Derek asked, standing and extending a hand to Joya.

She slid easily into his embrace, but had to stand on tiptoe to wrap her arms around his neck. He pulled her gently against him until she felt every lean delicious inch of him. The smell of his heady cologne and the champagne she'd drunk worked its magic. She was floating.

Being with Derek was beginning to feel right. He had so many of the qualities she admired in a man. He was good-looking, kind, intelligent and a good lover. A damn good lover, she reminded herself. So how come she couldn't get past his lack of ambition? A laid-back attitude didn't pay bills. But tonight she was willing to forget his shortcomings.

The slow dance ended and a livelier tune came on. The band brought in from Pelican Island began playing the Electric Slide and got the remaining guests up and moving. Even after the song ended, Rowan and Emilie remained on the floor. Emilie was up for a major grilling later.

Girlfriend came bounding toward her. "Come with me to the ladies' room," she said, taking Joya's arm. "We'll use the one downstairs in the lobby to avoid a line."

"Okay."

They'd completed their business and were standing at the mirror retouching their makeup when Emilie asked, "What's the deal with you and Derek?"

"What's with you and Rowan?"

Emilie calmly finished applying her lipstick and

tossed the tube back in her purse. She pressed her lips together. "Rowan's my date."

"Derek's my date."

"Smart ass. What I want to know is if you've slept with him yet?"

"MYOB," Joya warned, wagging a finger.

"Don't tell me to mind my own business. You're the one who said you didn't want to get involved with a blue-collar worker and changed your mind."

"Derek's working on Gran's store and we happen to get along," Joya said tightly. "That's it. He's not what I would call relationship material."

"You stupid, stupid girls. You don't know a good thing when it comes along," a woman's accented voice said from behind them. "That man is one helluva catch."

Camille Lewis stood washing her hands in a nearby sink. She was the last person they'd expected to see. She hadn't been at the wedding, which wasn't a surprise since Chere despised Camille and made no secret of it.

The gossip dried her hands on a monogrammed towel and eyed their outfits.

"What's the reception like? Tacky like the bride? Winston and I weren't invited, but we decided to have dinner here so that we could check out the place."

Just as Joya had thought: Camille, who hated to be left out of anything, was there to spy.

"Everything's been lovely and we're having a good time," she answered, eager to end the conversation and return to the reception. She picked up her purse.

"Derek was who you were talking about, right?" Camille asked, getting in her face. "Did you know he left a good engineering job to come back and work construction? What a waste of two master's degrees."

Her words stopped Joya from pushing by her. "What are you talking about?"

"Derek has advanced degrees in engineering and architecture. He was a senior engineer for some big company in the midwest. That boy had a wife, house, luxury automobile, the whole nine yards. He's not your average construction beefcake."

Joya's mouth hung open as Camille droned on, talking about how much money Derek used to make. Emilie quickly stepped in to take control.

"We need to go," she said.

But Camille was only warming up. She made no attempt to get out of Joya's face.

"That boy's parents were so poor they moved up north to live with relatives. He worked hard and made something of himself, and now he's thrown it all in to come back and fix up that dilapidated house his great-grandmother owns. He thinks it's going to improve the value, but I'm not sure Belle wants to sell."

Talk about being dumb. All the telltale signs

were there. Derek was polished and knew how to interact with all kinds of people. He had definite leadership skills.

"You could find worse relationship material," Camille said snidely. "I got to get back to Winston."

Emilie had Joya by the elbow, easing her from the room. She was in a daze, struggling to process this new information. It was she who hadn't realized her full potential. She had that undergraduate degree in speech therapy that she'd done nothing with. Derek was the one with the two advanced degrees who'd made something of himself. Could she trust what Camille had said?

"Bye, Camille," Emilie said, firmly.

As they were leaving a bathroom stall pushed open. Sheena, one of the bridesmaids emerged. She emptied a purse filled with cosmetics on the counter and found her blush.

"Upstairs was a little too crowded for my liking," she said, picking up a mascara wand. "Know what I mean?"

"Yep," Emilie acknowledged, whisking Joya away.

Derek was talking to Rowan when the women returned. The men stood and pulled out the women's chairs. Joya managed a vacant smile as a zillion thoughts raced through her head.

"Is everything okay?" Derek asked, frowning. He must be picking up something from her body language.

"What? Oh, yes, fine." Joya struggled to regroup. She'd already started looking at Derek in a different light. Did that make her superficial? She'd thought he wasn't what she wanted. Now she wasn't so sure.

Somehow she managed to get through the next hour, answering when she was spoken to, dancing when she was asked.

Sheena came over to ask Derek to dance and ended up making a public spectacle on the floor. Joya pretended it didn't annoy her, but she was relieved when Derek proposed they called it a night. They said their goodbyes and dutifully stopped by the bride and groom's table to hand them their gifts. To Joya's surprise Chere threw her arms around her and hugged her close.

"Thanks for coming, girl," she said in a loud whisper. "Don't let Sheena move in on Derek. She's my friend but she's a snake."

"Chere!" Quen admonished, indulgently.

"You know what I say is the truth. She tried hitting on you, didn't she?"

"Enjoy your honeymoon in the Bahamas," Joya said tactfully. Quen had his hands full.

"Thanks, I'm glad you came." He surprised her by hugging her. "We'll be in touch when we get back."

Outside, Derek said, "You're sure you're okay? You seem a little uncomfortable."

"It's been a tough night."

"Want to find some place quiet for a nightcap? I'm a good listener."

"I want to go home." Joya could tell by the way his lips pressed together he was disappointed by her answer. "You can come up for a drink."

The invitation made him brighten considerably.

Although her head was still spinning, she did not want to be alone. There was something about Derek that was quietly reassuring. He was steady and would be a good sounding board.

She waited until they were on the balcony of her apartment, sipping on cognac and enjoying the night, to say something. Derek was staring out onto the deserted boardwalk and had an arm draped loosely around her.

"Thanks for agreeing to come with me," she said, "It was a nice wedding."

"And you held up remarkably well. Thanks for being the perfect date." He kissed her right on the lips.

A small flutter began somewhere in her stomach and made her heart jump, even her toes tingled. She was dying to ask him if Camille had the skinny on him, but she didn't want him to think she'd been gossiping. "How long before the renovations at the store are done?"

"In another week or so. How's my quilt coming?"

"Getting there. I've been concentrating on it every chance I get. It's a joint effort so we're all working on individual blocks."

Derek drew her even closer. "You *are* coming to Nana's party, right?"

"Gran's coming."

"And you're not?" He looked at her as if he were disappointed, as if her being there would make or break his day. "You're the one recreating Belle's life on cloth. I can't believe you'd let an old lady down. Wouldn't you want to see her expression when she unwraps her gift?"

The initial flutter disappeared. She'd hoped Derek was asking, because he wanted her there.

"I may come for a while," she said, less than enthusiastically.

Derek nibbled on her earlobe. "Come for a long while. Stay for the whole party. Be my date."

The invitation left her heady. Breathless. She leaned over and kissed his cheek. Derek moved his head slightly and their lips connected. Joya was instantly on fire. A second kiss followed, and soon they were kissing with an intensity fueled by passion and way too much champagne.

The glasses of cognac were set on the patio table as they continued to embrace. One of Derek's hands caressed Joya's bare back, kneading her flesh, the other cupped her buttocks. When he brought her up against him he was already erect.

"We should go inside," Joya said, slipping out of the circle of his arms.

"Okay."

"I want you to spend the night," she said boldly, as Derek nibbled her bare shoulder and jiggled her zipper up and down.

"Okay."

"Is that all you can say? We're giving the town an X-rated show so it's not okay?"

She crooked a finger at him and Derek followed her inside and down the long hallway. Thank God she'd picked up the room before leaving for the wedding. She'd also turned on the air conditioner, making it nice and cool, and the linens were fresh.

Derek was already shedding his clothing. He'd left a trail behind him and now he stood bare-chested. She ran her hand across his hard chest, weaving her fingers through the coarse mat of hair covering his pectorals. She felt the muscles jump under her hand and tweaked a nipple.

He yanked on her zipper, a not-so-subtle sign that he wanted her out of her clothing. Joya pulled the dress over her head and tossed it on the floor.

"Nice thong panties," Derek commented as Joya prepared to strip them off. "Come here, you."

She came toward him in slow motion, working it and giving it all she had.

He had her off her feet in two seconds and on her back in bed. He was still wearing his pants when he straddled her. Joya opened Derek's zipper and reached inside his underpants. He groaned and removed a square package from his pocket, tossing the condom on the pillow.

Joya took him into her mouth, almost inhaling him. A deep guttural sound ripped from Derek's throat. His eyes were wide open but glazed over. And as she continued to work on him he left the world of reality behind.

She needed to get there with him. Joya shifted position. She felt the nip of teeth as he pushed the scrap of lace covering her pubis away. The tip of Derek's tongue circled and plunged. Joya moaned and her body felt ripe and heavy.

"I want you to love me," she said.

"I'm already doing that," he teased.

"I want you inside me."

Derek took the condom from the pillow where he had placed it. "Help me to get this on."

She helped him roll the condom on. By then they were both close to exploding. She eased herself on top of him and he entered her slowly. They began a rhythmical dance. He touched her and she touched him back, matching each other move for move, taking and giving pleasure.

Ankles firmly locked in place, their breathing synchronized. And as Derek gave a final thrust, in a defining moment of clarity Joya came to realize that Derek Morse had firmly implanted himself under her skin.

Chapter 16

"Miss Joya, you think I could talk to you for a minute?"

"What is it, Portia?"

Joya looked up from wiping down one of the newly built shelves in the showroom to see the student hovering. She'd been trying to get organized, but she was acutely aware of Derek halfway up a ladder replacing an electrical fixture. His proximity made her all jittery inside.

"Deborah asked me to ask you if she can get her job back. You said now we're busy we might need additional help so I'm asking. She knows the ropes."

"Forget it. There is no way I'm hiring her back."

"She'll work hard. She promised."

Joya caught Derek's almost imperceptible shake of his head and tried not to smile. She didn't need reminding. It would be a cold day in Flamingo Beach before she would rehire that lazy woman.

"Don't forget I might be leaving to go away to school. You'll need somebody," Portia whined.

"I'm sure I'll find somebody. I'll run an ad in the newspaper or put a sign out front."

Portia looked visibly put out but she went off to help a customer who'd just entered.

It was almost two weeks since Quen and Chere's wedding and the renovations were almost completed. There were only a few final touches and they would be done soon. Derek, rather than delegating to one of his men, had stayed on to work on them himself.

Even Granny J loved what he'd done. She was feeling much better and liked roaming around the homey interior, admiring the shiny new cash register and credit-card-processing machine. She would slowly climb the stairs to the loft and stand looking down on the colorful collage of quilts on display. And she kept singing Derek's praises.

With a centennial fast approaching, the town was attracting more and more tourists. And that meant an increase in revenue for Joya's Quilts. Tourists were literally coming in droves to Flamingo Beach. And all the hotels were overbooked. Several residents, seeing a money-making opportunity, were sprucing up their houses to turn them into bed and breakfasts. Those less enterprising slapped on coats of paint and concentrated on their gardens.

Flamingos had sprung up all over town. Joya, with Chet's help, had managed to get one erected on their joint property line. Granny J had made the bird a quilted cape and hood in a vivid lime green and mocha, and Chet and Harley had added a basket filled with flowers that the flamingo carried in its beak. That bird and its wild outfit was driving business into both of their stores. Derek named the flamingo Big Bird from the Hood.

"You're about to get visitors," Derek called from his perch up above.

"As long as they're here to spend money," Joya muttered back.

"Not those two."

"Uh-oh."

Joya glanced through the newly installed picture windows to see Lionel and Greg hurrying up the walkway.

"I'll be close by," Derek reminded her, taking a seat on the top rung of the ladder. "You stay cool."

She blew him a kiss. Since the night of the wedding they'd seen each other practically every day during work and off the premises. They'd concluded they were good in the bedroom and good at working out problems. Joya had come to rely on Derek for emotional support. She'd already discussed with him her need to find a job. Granny J would be chomping at the bit to run the show again—she already was.

Joya met Lionel and Greg at the front door.

"Hey guys, what's up?" she asked, noting their serious faces.

"We may have a lead," Greg said.

"What's with the police car?" Granny J called in a sleepy voice. She'd fallen asleep on the front porch. "Do we have a problem?"

"No problem, Gran."

The old lady slowly made her way inside. "Then why are you here?" she asked the two officers.

"Maybe we should go into the office," Joya suggested, mindful of the few customers browsing. She led the way to the room that had once been used for inventory but now was an office, complete with seating, computer and printer.

Joya made sure Granny J was off her feet before waving the men into chairs.

"Okay, so what's up?"

"Darnell came to see us," Greg said. "He had quite the story to tell."

"Darnell who used to spend most of his time in

front of the liquor store hitting everyone up for fifty cents to buy his pint?"

"That Darnell," Lionel said solemnly.

"What did Darnell have to say?" Gran asked. "He wasn't always a drunk, only took to drinking after he lost his wife to breast cancer. Up until then he was a sensible man."

"He said that someone is paying the gangs to make trouble for you." This came from Lionel.

Joya's eyebrows rose. "Flamingo Beach has gangs?"

"Things are changing. They come in from Pelican Island and the surrounding towns."

"And why would they target a quilt store of all places, when there are so many other stores to choose from?"

"It's not the quilt store, but the owner," Greg said patiently.

"But my grandmother's a popular woman."

"I am," Granny J huffed. "There's not a family in this town I don't know except for the newcomers moving in."

"But you aren't," Greg said bluntly. "You returned to town and for someone that's a threat. Maybe you're dating someone somebody else wants."

"I'm not dating anyone."

Lionel jutted a finger in the direction of the outer room. "What about him?"

"Derek? He and I are just good friends."

"That's not what's rumored. Anyway, we're going to be on the lookout for gangs in the general area. Be sure to lock up carefully and put on your security alarm when you go out."

Joya wanted to tell Lionel not to poke his nose in her business. But these two were pretty much the only game in town. Given the town's size you had to depend on them for everything and she didn't need to alienate them.

She thanked both police officers and escorted them to the door, promising to be especially vigilant for large groups of young people roaming in the area or entering the store. Granny J trailed her.

As she shut the door firmly behind them she heard Granny J saying to Derek, "Well I never. Fancy those two suggesting that my Joya moved in on someone's man, and that's why we're having the trouble we have."

"Did they say that now?" Derek drawled, still up on his ladder. "And who would that man be?"

Granny J drew her tiny body up so that instead of five feet nothing she looked like a six-foot Amazon. She wagged a finger at Derek. "My granddaughter is saving herself for someone special and I know just the man. He's a doctor and cute to boot. He's going to be taking her out soon."

"Granny J!" Joya called, charging back into the room in time to see the tense expression on Derek's face.

"Granny J nothing. Get on the phone and call up Dr. Ben. He's expecting to hear from you." She gave Derek a sly smile.

Joya noticed the tightness around Derek's mouth. Maybe she was a fool. But she was happy with the way things were going between them. She didn't see the need to bring another man into the mix.

"That woman telephoned you," Nana Belle shouted from her room the minute Derek let himself in the front door.

"What woman?" Derek called back, still irritated by the suggestion that Joya might be playing him. He had a sneaking suspicion he already knew who was on the other end of the line.

"The one chasing you. That Sheena, the neighborhood ho."

Derek exhaled a loud breath. Sheena had called at least ten times since he'd danced with her at the wedding. She'd wanted to go out, but he kept making excuses.

"Fine, I'll call her back. You saved the number?"

"Mari has it written down somewhere."

Derek continued through the house stopping in

each room to admire his handiwork. There was painting and some electrical work left to be done, plus the yard needed landscaping. He had too much on his plate at the moment and would probably pay a couple of the guys to finish up. Those waterfront villas would soon demand all of his attention.

The phone rang, and someone picked up.

"Phone for you, Derek," Mari yelled.

Hmmm. Most people he wanted to talk to called him on his cell phone. He hoped it wasn't Sheena again.

He waited to get to his room to pick up.

"Hello."

"Hey, how come you haven't called me back?"

"Who is this?" The female voice sounded familiar.

"Sheena."

"I just walked in," he said. "Nana just gave me your message."

"Watcha doing tonight?"

"Painting a room."

"There's a good movie on at the theater."

He decided to play with her. "You going?"

"Only if you're coming along."

"I'm busy, Sheena."

"What is it? You don't like me or what?"

"Just busy."

"No you like that woman better, and she don't even like you."

"What woman?"

"That stewardess. The one running her granny's shop. You know what she said about you?"

"I'm not sure I want to hear."

Sheena proceeded to tell him anyway. Derek listened because he was too polite to hang up on her. He wondered if she was making it up. She was not painting a very pretty picture of a woman he liked, but was, in fact, confirming his first impressions of Joya. He'd first thought her shallow, superficial and self-centered.

"And then she said you were nothing more than a glorified handyman, but she would play you until the work on her grandmother's store got done. She's using you."

Derek had heard enough. "Goodbye, Sheena." He hung up and threw himself on the bed. He had a lot to think about. Maybe he should pull the plug on the friendship right now.

He and Joya had been moving slowly toward a relationship. They'd been getting to know each other, and he'd thought they connected on a number of different levels. He needed to talk to someone who'd known Joya when she was married to Quen. Preston Shore might be a good choice.

He thought about the letter his old company had sent him inviting him back. He should give a call to follow up. Maybe tomorrow. And tomorrow he would call Rowan James and set up lunch. He'd quite liked the man and thought they might work well together.

What he needed was a run to clear his head, followed by a long, cold shower. Afterward he'd call Preston to see if he would join him for a quick beer. It was really eating him up that the woman he'd come to like and admire might have her own agenda.

After pushing himself to the limits, Derek limped back to the house. He wasn't motivated to do much now, not the painting that needed doing, or the floors in the dining room that needed refinishing. He was done. Emotionally drained. Burned.

He gave a quick call to Preston.

"Hey guy, something wrong?" his boss and friend asked as soon as he picked up.

"I'm heading for the Haul Out. Want to come?"

"I'm in for the night."

"Just a quick one," Derek wheedled. "I'll walk. Meet you there."

"This is going to cost you. My wife's going to hand me my head on a plate."

They agreed to meet in twenty minutes.

Derek was tying the laces on his sneakers when Nana called to him.

"Where you going, boy?"

"Out."

"You not planning on getting drunk and coming back here loud and rowdy?"

"Of course not, Nana."

Nana Belle could be clairvoyant at times.

Needing time to think, Derek took the long way to the Haul Out. If what Sheena said was true, he should do the smart thing and put distance between himself and Joya. He was no one's plaything. It had never occurred to him that Joya might be using him for sex and to get her grandmother's store finished.

Too late. He was already involved. He'd developed feelings for the woman.

By the time he got to the bar he'd worked up a good head of steam. He elbowed his way through the crowded entrance, and navigated his way around the patrons bellying up to the bar. No sign of Preston so far. Derek ordered two beers on tap and took them with him to the side of the room where the regulars were watching three men and a woman play pool. He set one of the glasses down on a crowded table and tossed half his beer down in one easy swallow. Where the hell was Preston?

Derek gave it another couple of minutes before sucking down the other beer. He went back to the bar to replenish both glasses.

A woman who looked somewhat familiar sidled up to him.

"How about buying me a drink?" she said.

"What are you having?"

"Same thing as you."

It wasn't in his nature to be rude so he bought her a drink and concentrated on his.

"You're Derek Morse, right?"

"I am." By now his tongue was getting heavy.

"I'm LaTisha Clements."

An unusual name. A familiar name.

"I used to work at Joya's Quilts," she reminded him. "I've been watching you."

He remembered her, too. She and the other salesgirl were the two who'd kicked up a fuss in the front yard.

"So you knocking boots with that snotty bitch or what? Betcha I could take care of you better."

LaTisha brushed her hand across his jeans touching him in a place no stranger should touch.

"Uh, 'scuse me. Aren't you with someone?" he asked, thinking this was one brazen, crazy woman. Most men would have jumped on the invitation, but not him. He liked his women a heck of a lot more subtle and he liked them petite. Like Joya.

"My friends aren't here yet. Keep me company until they arrive."

"Derek?"

Preston had arrived, thank God. Derek didn't even bother saying goodbye, just turned and left.

He and Preston found a spot on the other side of the bar where they could sip their drinks and keep an eye on surroundings.

Finally Preston said, "So why did you drag me out at this hour? You got my wife thinking I'm cheating on her. We had one heck of an argument."

"What do you know about Joya Hamill?" There, he'd said it.

"The older Joya or the younger one?" Preston asked, keeping a straight face.

"Don't be a wise guy."

"The woman you wanted no part of because she was high-maintenance and you were sick of that type."

"You're being a jerk."

"Me? I only repeat what I hear. Okay, I'll tell you what I know. Joya grew up with her grandmother. Her parents were killed in a car accident when she was little and Granny J raised her. She went off to college, came back, fell in love with Quentin Abraham and married him."

"Yeah, yeah, I know all that. What's her personality like? Her reputation around town?"

"You've been spending time with her. Don't you know?"

"I need an objective opinion."

"You're in love," Preston teased. "Look at you. What happened?"

Derek took a good long pull on his beer. He'd had his confidence shaken and no longer trusted his judgment or instincts. He didn't want to seem like a wimp repeating word for word what Sheena had said.

"I'm thinking," he said slowly. "Now that the job at the quilt shop is almost completed I need to put some distance between myself and her."

"Any particular reason?"

"I wouldn't want her to think I'm looking to get serious. She needs a different kind of man."

Two women wearing itty-bitty shorts brushed by them. One of them stopped to say hi. Both men nodded and quickly returned to their conversation. Without the encouragement they were looking for the women moved on. When a couple of stools freed up at the bar, the men moved in. Derek signaled to the bartender and ordered them another round. So much for just having one beer.

"You're looking to get me in more trouble with my wife?" Preston joked as he knocked one back.

"No, I'm just looking for good advice. Experience has taught me when you're in a no-win situation you're better off making a clean break."

"What makes you believe you're in a situation you can't win?" Preston asked thoughtfully.

Derek screwed up his mouth, thinking. Finally he said, "I made the difficult decision to change my life.

I walked away from a six-figure salary to do what I wanted to do, which is work with my hands. I meet a woman that I like, I sensed she was high-maintenance from the get go, but I was willing to give it a try. And now it's been confirmed she's not looking for a construction worker. She's looking for a man on his way up or already there. I see the red flag waving in the wind. Heck, I would be a masochist to pursue her. I already had one materialistic woman in my life trying to change me."

Preston took another gulp of beer. "You make a good point, so what are you going to do?"

"I'm done," Derek said, setting down his glass as the room around him began to blur. "I'm moving on."

"So who's the next candidate? Someone in this bar?"

Derek glared at him.

Preston stared back. He slid off his stool and reached for his wallet. "I got to get home. If not you'll be testifying for me in divorce court. Coming?"

"I'll be along in a while."

"Should I take your car keys from you?"

"I told you I walked," Derek said.

Preston threw some bills on the bar. "Try not to get too drunk then," he said, heading off in the direction of the exit.

Derek already had a finger up, signaling the bartender to fill him up.

Chapter 17

"I haven't heard from Derek in at least a week," Joya confided as she and Emilie sat side by side enjoying a pedicure—Emilie's treat. "He may be giving me the cold shoulder and I'm not sure why. I miss him."

"Why don't you call him?" Emilie answered distracted, as she leafed through a magazine.

"I've tried. He hasn't returned one call. He'll have to come out of hiding soon because there's his Nana's quilt to pick up and the party is next week. He decided to have it at the house after all."

"Didn't he ask you to be his date?"

Joya shrugged. "Guess he forgot. I don't understand men."

Emilie had planned this girlfriend day out. She'd used her corporate privileges at the Flamingo Beach Spa Resort to get them various services and treatments. So far, they'd had deep-tissue massages and a seaweed wrap. Now they were relaxing and thoroughly enjoying their pedicures. Next on the agenda was lunch at the resort's elegant bistro.

The attendant at Joya's feet painted her little toe a summery pink.

"What do you think?" she asked.

"I like it. Makes me feel young again."

Emilie who'd settled on a fire-engine-red polish was being led to an area to dry her toes. Joya soon joined her. They sipped on cups of tea and the conversation resumed.

"So what do you think is really going on with Derek?" Emilie asked.

Joya snorted. "Maybe he started dating someone and didn't know how to tell me."

"And that's the kind of man you want to be with? The type who isn't brave enough or classy enough to let you know when a relationship is over with?" Emilie added sarcastically.

"But we weren't really dating."

"You were spending a lot of time together and that constitutes a relationship to me."

"I guess he thought differently."

"Well he can't avoid you forever, not in a town this size. Why don't you show up somewhere where you know he's going to be and try talking to him?"

"Confront him?" What an outrageous idea. She'd never been one of those women. "Can you imagine me walking onto the site and insisting he speak with me?"

"Why not? He's working on those new waterfront villas right here on the property. You could say that you'd been calling to speak to him about the quilt, and since he hasn't returned your calls you came to find him in person."

"It's too much energy to put out. I'll have to think about it."

"I'm hungry," Emilie said, setting down the cup of herbal tea the attendant had given her. "How about you?"

"Starving."

"We'll give it another five minutes with these toes and then off to lunch we go."

Derek had agreed to meet Rowan James for lunch at Beachcombers, the resort's bistro. The two men had hit it off at Chere and Quen's wedding. Somehow, the developer had found out about Derek's advanced degrees in engineering and architecture and he'd proposed they talk.

Derek wasn't sure exactly what *talk* meant, but he sure was going to keep all of his options open. He had some serious decisions to make in the next few weeks. He'd called his old company and was assured they wanted him back tomorrow. The package they were offering was almost impossible to refuse.

Curious as to why Rowan wanted to meet, Derek had left the construction site and taken the time to clean up, even using the resort bathroom to change clothes and swap his dusty boots for a pair of loafers.

Refusing to think about Joya, he'd buried himself in work this last week, putting in long hours. He'd brought in help to finish up Nana Belle's house, but he'd also ended up working alongside the guys. All in all, it had paid off, the project was finally near completion and the house would be done in time for the party.

And a good thing, too, the centennial celebrations were right round the corner and everyone was fixing up their places. Traffic had picked up and there was congestion everywhere you turned. Derek had never seen so many signs for grand openings in his life. Any establishment that could slap on a coat of paint was having a grand opening and inviting people to come in to browse and have tropical drinks.

"Can I seat you, sir?" the hostess at the entrance asked as Derek continued to pace.

"I'm waiting for someone."

"Perhaps your party is already seated," she said. "Give me their name."

Derek did so and she consulted a computer.

"Yes, Mr. James is already here. Shall I take you to him?"

He followed the slender young woman to the table where Rowan was seated.

"Hey, guy," Rowan said, rising and meeting him halfway. They pumped hands and Derek took the seat Rowan waved him into.

Rowan's finger was in the air summoning the waiter. "What are you drinking?" he asked.

"Water. I have to get back to work."

"Two bottled waters then and menus."

The waiter scurried off to get their order and Rowan chewed on a breadstick thoughtfully. "You're probably wondering why I invited you to lunch."

"The thought did cross my mind."

"It's like this," Rowan said starting in. "I am considered a developer with deep pockets but I'm still an outsider. And I'm from up north, which makes me even more suspicious. You're the local boy made good. You got out, got degrees, did the corporate thing, and came back to work with your hands. These people trust you and you understand them."

"Yes…and?"

"You're good partnership material."

"I'm not sure I understand."

The waiter handed them menus and water. "I'll give you gentlemen a few minutes," he said, leaving them again.

"Give us ten." When he was out of earshot, Rowan continued. "Land developers travel, which means we aren't always there to keep an eye on things. Plus, and this is strictly confidential now, we usually don't know Jack about construction, which means we often get taken. You're the kind of guy who can straddle the fence, going from T-shirt to suit, plus, you know the people and understand their mentality."

Derek was getting it quick. Even so, his loyalty kicked in. "I work for Shore Construction," he reminded Rowan. "Preston Shore gave me a chance when most wouldn't. No one thought I wanted to get my hands dirty."

The developer dismissed his comment with another wave of his hand. "Preston's a decent guy and a businessman. If the shoe were on the other foot—well…anyway a big birdie told me you're on board to learn the business from the ground up. You're ambitious and looking to start up your own construction company. True?"

"True."

"Then you must know start-ups cost money. You'll need funding, plus it takes time to build a business. What I'm proposing wouldn't cost you a dime out of pocket. And the salary I'm willing to pay is more than you could ever make hauling cement."

Rowan named a figure.

Derek whistled. The whole package would be difficult to turn down. His head was spinning.

Rowan let loose with a long low whistle of his own. "It's our lucky day. Look who just walked in. Emilie Woodward gets my engines revving and her friend, the one you were with at the wedding, is pretty damn hot."

With an anticipatory flutter in the pit of his stomach, Derek gazed in the direction Rowan was staring. He had been dreading the moment when he had to face Joya and had been lying low. He'd needed space and time to get over his hurt feelings. And he still couldn't understand why she kept calling. Her grandmother's place was done.

"Let's table the discussion for now. Think over everything I've said." Rowan stood up. "I'm going to ask the ladies to join us."

Rowan was off in the direction of the women.

This was going to be awkward. But at least there would be other people around. Minutes later Rowan returned, making a face. "They turned me down flat. This is a girlfriends' outing, like I'm supposed to know what that means. I guess they'd rather eat with each other than dine with us. I would have picked up the tab." His laughter was hollow. He didn't like being rejected.

Someone was looking out for him. Oh no, Emilie Woodward was coming over.

"We'll join you for coffee and dessert," she said breezily.

"We'll look forward to it," Rowan said, rallying. He beamed as she walked away as though she'd just handed him a million dollars. "Guess I still have it. Unless it's you she likes."

Their waiter was back. Derek stabbed a finger at the menu. His appetite had returned. "Burger and fries. I'm not going to be able to stay for dessert."

"What?"

"I need to get back to work."

"Okay, since you and Joya are dating you get to see her any time, I guess."

"We're not dating," Derek said stiffly.

"Could have fooled me."

But Derek's eyes kept darting over to the area

where the ladies lunched. Joya, dressed in a short skirt and cute little halter top, was making him hungry, and not just for lunch.

He managed to wolf down his meal when it was brought to him, then quickly shot out of his chair.

"Thanks, Rowan, I'll be in touch and let you know one way or the other."

The men shook hands and Rowan handed him his business card again. "Let me know something definitive by next week," Rowan added. "I need to finalize travel plans."

"You'll have an answer in a few days."

Derek made it to the entrance before he heard heels tip-tapping behind him.

"Derek, can you wait up for a moment?" Joya called.

He couldn't continue walking, that would be just too rude.

"Oh, hi Joya."

She stood directly in his path, scanning his face. "Is there something wrong between us?"

"Why do you say that?

"I haven't seen you in some time. You haven't returned my calls. It made me wonder."

"I'm just busy. You know how it is." He felt like a louse.

She looked at him with those wide gray eyes and he got the feeling she didn't believe a word he said.

"Your grandmother's quilt is ready," Joya said, quietly. "Let me know what you want to do about it. If you prefer, I can make arrangements for Granny J or someone else to bring it to you."

He felt like an even bigger dirt bag. He'd invited her to be his date at Nana's party and she was providing an easy way out. Maybe instead of letting it fester, he should just tell her what was eating him up.

"Joya..."

But she'd already walked away. And although he wanted to stop her, pride got in the way.

Joya got back to her place to find a message from Dr. Benjamin on the answering machine. He left her a number that she assumed must be his office. Since Granny J had gone in for a check-up earlier that week Joya immediately assumed the worse.

She took a deep breath before picking up the receiver and punching in the number. Might as well get it over with.

A receptionist answered and she was put on hold.

"Dr. Benjamin," the doctor said in his no-nonsense manner sounding somewhat distracted.

"It's Joya Hamill, Granny J's granddaughter. You asked me to call. Is everything okay with my grandmother?"

"Oh, Joya. Thanks for calling back. Yes, yes, your

grandmother is coming along nicely. My call was more of a personal nature."

"Oh!" she waited, wondering if Granny J was up to it again.

"I thought perhaps if you weren't busy that you might be interested in accompanying me to the cocktail party at Mayor Rabinowitz's mansion. It's the event that kicks off the centennial celebrations. The one where they're conducting that silent auction for the flamingos around town."

"When is it?" Joya asked, carefully.

"Next Friday."

And Saturday was Belle's party. Dr. Ben had caught her completely off guard and she couldn't think of a good excuse to turn him down. Besides, he seemed a nice enough man and an invitation to the mayor's mansion was nothing to sneeze at. She hadn't heard of him dating anyone local, and he wasn't married either, which were both good things. Plus, the way it looked, she and Derek were done. Not that they'd been dating. She was as free as a bird.

"Sure I'd love to attend and thank you for asking."

"Good. Good. I'll call again closer to the date to give you the particulars."

Joya thanked him and hung up. She should have been elated. Dr. Kyle Benjamin was more in line with what she thought she wanted, but how come she didn't feel the least bit excited about the date they'd just set up?

An annoying voice at the back of her mind gave her the answer. Because what she'd done was fallen in love with Derek Morse.

And Derek was one hard act to follow.

Chapter 18

Granny J was back to form, bustling around the newly refurbished store like her old self when Joya returned from the bank. She was feeling much better now that sawdust wasn't constantly in the air and paint fumes didn't make her gag.

"You do your own dirty work. Don't hand it off to that child," Gran said, thrusting at her one of the big yellow shopping bags that Joya had had specially made up to advertise the store. It read: Joya's Quilts—Providing Coverage for Another Hundred Years.

Inside was Nana Belle's commemorative quilt. Joya had asked Portia to deliver it to the Flamingo

Beach Resort and Spa where Derek was working, and it was still sitting here.

"That quilt needs to get to Derek before tomorrow. He's going to want to examine it and probably gift-wrap it before his great-grandmother's party," Joya reminded Gran.

"In that case, you pick up the phone and call him to come by and get it."

Joya made a wry face. "I can't do that."

"Why not?"

"I don't think he wants to see me."

"Enough of this childish behavior," Granny J said. "The two of you are acting like two lovestruck teenagers."

"Hardly lovestruck."

"Then act like adults, face up to your problems and talk things out. You *are* planning on showing up at his great-grandmother's party with me tomorrow?"

Joya huffed out a breath. "I'm still thinking about it. Going out two nights in a row might just wear me out."

"That's right, you have a date with Dr. Benjamin."

"We're going to the mayor's cocktail party this evening."

"What are you wearing?"

Joya shrugged. She hadn't given much thought to any of it and although she wanted to feel excited she just couldn't. The party was a big deal: anyone who was anybody had been invited. It was the kickoff to an entire month of celebration. Since it wasn't every day that a town turned one hundred years old they were breaking out all the stops. There were tall ships in the harbor and every vendor was selling some kind of souvenir.

"Gran," Joya said changing the subject, "There's something I've been meaning to talk to you about."

"Sounds serious," Granny J said, taking a seat on one of the newly upholstered couches.

"When you were in the hospital and I had to do the banking I found out you took out an equity loan. Why?"

"The store was all paid for. Why not?"

"Why did you need the money, Gran?"

The old lady pursed her lips and studied her knuckles, then she reluctantly said, "The store wasn't making a profit. It cost money to keep it open and pay salaries and I was determined not to go bankrupt. This store has been in our family for years."

"I understand, hon. Since the store's doing better now you should be able to pay down that loan. What's that smell?" Joya sniffed the air.

"Smells like something's on fire."

The conversation was tabled as both women raced toward the back room, Joya leading the way.

"Call the fire department," Joya shouted, spotting

the smoke seeping through a closed door. "The supply room is on fire."

In the distance, sirens could be heard. A glance out the window indicated a small crowd had already gathered on the sidewalk.

Harley Mancini came charging in. "Chet spotted the smoke. We didn't bother calling you figuring what could you do about it? The fire department is on its way. You need to get out."

He grabbed both women by the elbows and began moving them toward the door. He was dragging them down the walkway when the fire truck pulled up and the firefighters, dragging hoses, leapt out.

All Joya could think about was the mess that would have to be cleaned up in the newly renovated store. The firefighters were bound to track in dirt on their boots and leave smudgy fingerprints on the walls, not to mention the water damage. But it was better than having the place burn down.

In minutes, the fire, which was said to have been caused by a cigarette, was put out. Neither she nor Granny J smoked.

"Arson," Chet insisted, confronting one of the firefighters. "You need to check that angle out. The fire had to have been set deliberately."

"We've already notified the police."

At that moment Greg and Lionel came screeching up in their cop car, siren going.

"Clear the way," they ordered, racing out and attempting to take control.

What followed for the next couple of hours was a total blur. People were questioned and firefighters and a detective tromped in and out. The cigarette that was the cause of the problem was taken away for evidence. It was one of those menthol brands.

Luckily the damage was minor: just a couple of quilts destroyed but they were favorites. One had a Flying Geese pattern and another had a Card Trick block. But overall, a good airing out and a new coat of paint would fix the damage. Thank goodness for insurance.

By the time everyone had finally cleared out, Joya was exhausted and the cocktail party was only hours away.

"I'm tempted not to go," she said to Granny J. "I don't want to leave you alone, and, frankly, I'm in no mood to go to a party."

"I'll be fine and you have a date. You can't possibly cancel at this last minute. Go home and make yourself pretty. A couple of the women from the guild are coming over and we'll be working on more commemorative quilts. Sales have been great, so better to have too many than too little, don't you think?"

"Okay, but only if you're sure."

Joya's cell phone rang as she was hustling out of the door.

"Good. You're okay. I just heard about the fire," Derek's voice rushed out at her making her stomach flutter. "I'm on my way over."

"No need to be. Everything's under control."

"No one was hurt then? What about damage?"

"Minor actually. The fire was set in the supply room."

"Set? What do you mean set?" Derek asked.

"It was deliberate. The firefighters found a smoldering cigarette. None of us smoke."

"I don't like what I'm hearing."

"Neither do I. But listen, I have to run. Your nana's quilt's done. What do you want me to do with it?"

"Hold onto it," Derek said, surprising her. "I'll come by your place either later or tomorrow to pay you and pick it up."

"What about wrapping and that kind of thing?"

"I'll just hang it on the wall so that when Nana is wheeled in it's the first thing she sees."

"Good idea. Call me before you come. I may not be home."

Joya retraced her steps to retrieve the bag holding the quilt.

"Changed your mind, I see," Granny J said dryly.

"I'm a woman, I have that prerogative," Joya said giving her grandmother a saucy wink. "No doubt you'll be calling me later to see how my date went."

"Probably not. I already have a pretty good idea how it will go. Now go, child. You're already running late."

Somehow she managed to make it across town and get herself together in less than an hour. The function, she'd been told, was semi-formal, and so she opted for a simple spaghetti-strapped cocktail dress in burnt orange that had a matching clutch purse. She pulled the whole thing together with a double strand of black pearls, earrings and her signature heels.

Rather than stay in her apartment, she would go downstairs to the lobby to wait for Kyle Benjamin.

His gray Lexus pulled up to the front of the building at the agreed-upon time. The doctor, dressed in a well-cut taupe suit stepped out of his vehicle and into the building. He carried a small wrapped box in one hand. He beamed when he saw Joya seated, waiting.

"You look lovely," he said, offering her his hand. "That color is great on you."

Joya thanked him and accepted the box he handed her.

"Should I open it now?" she asked.

"Yes, you can do so in the car. It would go perfectly with your dress."

When she was seated in his vehicle she undid the colorful ribbon on the box before lifting the lid.

"This is really lovely," she said, removing the two orchids that had been made into a corsage. Their mocha-and-cream centers complemented the orange of her dress.

Without being asked, Kyle reached across and took the corsage from her. "Wrist, shoulder or hair?" he asked.

She hadn't had a corsage since her senior high prom. "Hair," she said, feeling daring.

"How about right behind the ear? It worked for Billie Holiday and should work even better on you."

He was flirting with her, she realized. But she didn't have that immediate comfortable ease that she'd had with Derek, nor did she feel as if she couldn't wait to jump his bones. Kyle Benjamin would be good company and attentive to boot. He'd be the kind of guy a woman would want to be seen with, a pleasant companion but nothing more.

Joya allowed him to tuck the flower behind her ear. But even though his fingers lightly grazed her flesh she felt nothing. He could just as easily have been her brother.

The mayor's mansion was in one of the older country-club communities. Several harried valets were attempting to park cars when they arrived. Uniformed police, borrowed from the neighboring towns, supplemented Flamingo Beach's limited force and provided security. Greg and Lionel, not ones to miss out on an opportunity, had stationed themselves at the mansion's entrance.

"How about I drop you off at the front door?" Kyle proposed. "It may be a while before we see a valet."

"That would be fine." Joya did not relish having to walk any distance in heels that were more stylish than practical. "I'll meet you here in a few minutes," he said taking off.

She walked up to the front entrance along with several women whose escorts had dropped them off. Lionel and Greg were checking invitations and identifications despite knowing most of the guests personally.

"My date has my invitation," Joya said when it was her turn. "He's parking the car."

"He's already inside," Greg said, winking at her. "You look hot, girl." His eyes traveled the length of her.

"Thanks, but Kyle couldn't possibly be here already. He dropped me off and is parking the car."

"Better take that size-twelve hoof out of your mouth," Lionel guffawed, elbowing his partner playfully in the gut. "Joya's not here with Derek."

The sound of Derek's name made Joya's pulse

race and her heartbeat escalate. In her wildest dreams she hadn't expected to see him here. Then she sobered, realizing that he probably wasn't alone. She couldn't bear seeing him with another woman. But maybe he'd come stag, or why would Greg assume she was his date?

More people flowed in, some of whom she knew and some of whom were from out of town. Joya exchanged greetings and the necessary small talk with a few until she spotted Kyle at the entrance. He scanned the area looking for her while Greg and Lionel examined his invitation.

Joya waved and he came over.

"Did you find some place to park?" she asked.

"Yes, eventually. It's way out in the boonies, but at least I'm assured of not having my vehicle nicked. After that long walk I do need a drink." When Joya gave him a sideways look he added, "I'm not on call for the next twenty-four hours. We can call the local taxi service if I get too inebriated. Now shall we go in and see who there is to meet?"

Taking her by the elbow, Kyle gently edged her inside the library where the function was being held. It was a cavernous space with sculptures strategically positioned on pedestals. Bookshelves filled with books rimmed the room and couches provided comfortable seating. Waiters and waitresses were doing their best to move back and forth carrying trays of drinks and hors d'oeuvres above their heads. The noise level was deafening. The poor string quartet playing off in a corner could barely be heard.

A number of fragrances filled the air. Joya inhaled the exotic spices and garlicky scents wafting over from the mini-burritos and shrimp on the trays. She inhaled the scent of expensive perfumes and colognes from the guests. A festive citrus-type drink was being served in tall chilled glasses adorned with little paper umbrellas. The tangy smell tickled her nostrils and made her long for one.

"My guess is the back patio's less crowded," Kyle said close to her ear as he steered her toward a door leading out to an Olympic-size pool.

He was right. It was far less congested outside. The large flagstone patio overlooking the golf course had a decent amount of people milling around the two bars but nowhere near the crowd inside. Red-white-and-blue flags adorned a gazebo that served as a stage. And a saxophonist roamed playing mood music, the perfect background sound for a group bent on circulating and networking.

Joya watched the guests make their rounds, stop to make small talk then move on when someone better caught their eye. All in all, it was a highbrow event. The men, for the most part, all wore suits and ties and were accompanied by glamorous women in everything from long flowing skirts to chic short dresses. Everyone's finery had been brought out.

A couple Joya had never seen before approached Kyle.

"Nice to see you out and about," the man said. He gave Joya a vague smile, nodding in her direction before holding out his hand.

"I'm Dr. Timothy Broderick and this is my wife, Dr. Samantha Chin."

Joya introduced herself and shook the hand of Dr. Broderick before clasping the slender hand of his Asian wife. She guessed them to be Kyle's colleagues from Flamingo Beach General. The men immediately began conversing leaving the women to find common ground.

"Call me Sam," Broderick's wife said.

"Sam it is. Take a look at this crowd. I thought I pretty much knew everyone there is to know in town, but a lot of these people are strangers."

"Yes, I know what you mean." Sam chuckled and Joya thought she was cool. She didn't seem at all stuck up or impressed with herself as some professionals tended to be. "How did you meet Kyle?" she asked.

"My grandmother is his patient."

"That lovely woman who owns Joya's Quilts? Duh!" she slapped her forehead. "You're the younger

Joya, the granddaughter Granny J speaks so fondly of, who's helping her run the store."

"You know my grandmother?"

Sam nodded. "Actually, I've bought several quilts from her. I hate to talk shop but do you think that it's too late to order a centennial quilt?"

"Just tell me what colors and your design preference and I'll make it happen. Do you have a particular price range in mind?"

Sam took a business card from her purse and scribbled. She handed Joya the card and Joya glanced at it before tucking it into her own purse.

"Consider it done."

"I don't know about you," Sam continued, "but I'm thirsty and these men of ours have forgotten their manners. Let's find a bar or a nice accommodating waiter." She waved at her husband. "Joya and I are off to find something to drink. We'll be back."

Joya was halfway across the patio before she spotted Derek. He was speaking to Rowan James and a couple of women hovered on the periphery. He did not see her and although she had no claims on him, it burned her that she might already have so easily been replaced.

"Something wrong?" Sam asked, turning back when she realized Joya's pace had slowed.

"No, I just stopped to say hello to someone I

knew," she lied. "There's a waiter. He's got champagne and that fun-looking citrus drink. Think we can make it over while he's still got drinks on that tray?"

"Wait, there's another tray circulating," Sam pointed out. "That waitress is a whole lot closer and she's got drinks."

"Okay, we're on our way."

But she couldn't shake the black feeling that had descended, and she couldn't help wishing that she'd come to the cocktail party with Derek and not Kyle Benjamin. She took a deep breath and accepted the concoction Sam handed her.

"Should we get something for the guys?" Joya asked.

"Heck, no! Let them find whatever they're drinking. If you noticed, they were so busy talking they forgot to be gentlemen." Sam took a long drag on her straw. "Ummm, delicious, tastes like there might be some passion fruit mixed in."

"Yoo hoo, Dr. Chin," an older woman, one of the town's matrons said, approaching and immediately beginning to ask questions about an upcoming surgery.

Realizing the conversation might go on forever, Joya excused herself and headed back to find Kyle.

Chapter 19

Derek was beginning to think it might have been a mistake to attend this cocktail party. He'd only agreed because Rowan had talked him into it. He'd said it was the perfect place to network and be seen.

But now he was stuck with this woman who was supposed to be his date. The problem was, she didn't have two brain cells to rub together. Rowan had set him up with one of his employees because he'd said it wouldn't be cool to arrive at the mayor's function alone.

Rowan had been forced to come up with a date as well because Emilie Woodward had turned him down flat. Right now Rowan was bristling because he'd spotted Emilie, who'd arrived with a reporter from the *Flamingo Beach Chronicle.*

Derek's date was definitely eye candy but not the brightest bulb in the room. She clutched his arm and was going on about all the important people she recognized and how impressed she was.

She was now telling him of her plan for getting Mayor Rabinowitz's autograph. This called for another drink, Derek decided. He glanced off in the direction of the nearest bar and spotted Joya walking toward him and damn near died. What was she doing here? He hadn't expected her.

Much as he'd tried to ignore it, he missed her. Missed their easy conversation and missed the feel and smell of her warm body next to his. Putting space between them hadn't been all bad though. It had given him time to think. And he'd realized that perhaps he'd been too quick to take Sheena's words as gospel. Based on the number of phone calls she'd made to him since, she clearly wasn't just using him to get her grandmother's shop renovated.

Rather than pouting, sulking and imagining the worst, what he needed to do was have a long-overdue conversation with Joya. Now was as good a time as any. Tomorrow was Nana's party that he'd worked so hard on. He should try to patch things up with Joya prior to that.

Derek wondered if Joya had seen him. If not, the element of surprise was on his side. He practically pried his date's hand off his arm. She had one of those showgirl names like Amber or Solange; he hadn't really been listening closely. What he did know was that she was trying her best to get him into bed.

"Excuse me," he said leaving her, "I'm going to freshen my drink. Can I get you something?"

"Another margarita might be nice."

"You got it." With that he took off.

Joya was still heading in his direction when he crossed paths with her. He was certain with a crowd this size she had not seen him. He loved the touch of the orchid behind her ear. Very Billie. Actually very Joya. And it hit him as though someone had taken a baseball bat to his head. He'd gone and fallen in love with this woman. And he'd sworn to never go there again.

"Fancy seeing you here," he said, "You never mentioned you were coming when we spoke earlier."

"Neither did you."

By her wild-eyed expression she was visibly shaken.

"Had you said something, we could have come together," Derek said.

Joya took a sip of her drink and pulled herself together. Slowly she appraised him. "I'm sorry, but I'm here with someone."

So it was like that. "I'm here with someone, too," Derek answered. "Frankly I'd rather be with you."

She continued to stare at him.

"May I have your attention," a voice boomed over a microphone. "In just a few minutes our honorable Mayor Solomon Rabinowitz will kick off our centennial celebration with a state-of-the-beach speech." The announcer chuckled at his own joke and several guests chuckled with him.

"I need to find my date," Joya said, preparing to retrace her steps.

"I'll stop by later for Nana's gift and we'll talk then. You took the quilt home with you?"

"Yes, but call me before you come."

She headed off, trotting right past him. Curious and more than a little jealous, although he would never willingly admit it, Derek looked over to see where she ended up.

A well-dressed man included Joya in his circle. He threw his arm around her shoulder and she laughed up at him. Derek recognized the popular Dr. Benjamin. He wanted to take his head off. He didn't know him personally, but he had heard he was popular with the ladies.

Joya had traded a humble construction worker for a medical doctor. No, he wasn't about to go down that road again and let the old insecurities take over. He was just as good as the next guy and in many ways had more to bring to the table. He could get down and dirty when he needed to, but he cleaned up real well, and could talk the talk. More important he walked the walk.

If Joya wanted a professional guy he could play the role. But first he needed to get things straight with her. He never should have listened to the malicious gossip of a woman who clearly had an ax to grind. He'd acted like an impetuous teenager instead of a grown man. Rather than addressing the situation up front he'd shut down and withdrawn.

People often said and did things they did not mean. He was the perfect example. He had sworn off personal involvements until his business was up and running, and he'd been determined not to get involved with any woman who screamed high-maintenance. And what he'd done was fallen hard for a woman who had nice things and expected to be treated decently. Joya wasn't necessarily greedy. She just thought highly of herself. Nothing wrong with that.

What he thought he wanted was not what he needed. It had taken him forever to realize that.

Derek gazed up at the mayor standing in the middle of his gazebo, red-white-and-blue flags fluttering behind his head. He forced himself to concentrate. Behind him a projection screen flashed an aerial view of Flamingo Beach with the heading, One Hundred Years Old and Still Going Strong.

Change was long overdue. Miriam Young, dubbed the Flip-Flop Momma because of the flip-flops she wore, should have been up there as mayor, not this guy who had been accused of skewing the ballot boxes, spewing rhetoric he thought everyone wanted to hear.

"What a pleasure it is to welcome you here this evening," Solomon Rabinowitz crowed to the crowd, arms extended as if he were welcoming children to the fold. "Today kicks off the start of a month-long celebration. In a few short weeks Flamingo Beach will celebrate its one-hundredth birthday."

Applause.

"During those years there have been many changes. We've watched our population grow in leaps and bounds. At the last official count we were up to eighteen hundred, and that figure changes every day as more and more people move into Flamingo Beach." The mayor opened his arms even wider. "Not many of us can say we lived to the ripe old age of one hundred except maybe Belle Carter, of whom we are all fond and whom some call Nana Belle." The mayor paused to acknowledge the loud outburst of applause which greeted Belle's name before continuing, "Despite trials, tribulations and hardships, Flamingo Beach has survived and thrived."

Another wild outburst of applause followed. The crowd, fortified by free drinks, was getting in the mood.

The mayor, figuring he now had the crowd, began to recount the floods of the early nineteen-hundreds which washed away most of the boardwalk and surrounding stilt houses. He talked of a fire in the nineteen-fifties reputed to have been started by the Ku Klux Klan that had taken out a number of the stores on the Row, and how the citizens had banded together, supporting each other during hard times.

"We are survivors," he said. "I can proudly say that for years this community has remained a community. When others had race riots our citizens stayed aligned, and our children played side by side. We are known as a conservative community, but we are not having the problems others have. Our children can still play outdoors. Your car doors for the most part remain unlocked, and when you see your neighbor on the street you look them directly in the eye and you say 'hello.' Now I'm turning my microphone over to our auctioneer who'll also announce the winner of the best dressed flamingo in town. Please join me in singing..." Mayor Rabinowitz paused for effect "...Happy Birthday, Flamingo Beach."

More applause followed. Derek had had enough. He began making his way back to where he'd left Rowan and his date. He had a big day tomorrow and he'd planned on turning in early. But first he had a quilt to pick up. He was going to Flamingo Place even if he had to sit in the parking lot and wait until the doctor dropped off Joya. If she planned on entertaining at home he'd have to be added to the invitation list. They'd wasted enough time.

Derek found his group and told them he needed to leave. A half hour later, still dressed in a business suit, he was parked in a visitor's spot at the condominium waiting for Joya.

He didn't have long to wait. A gray Lexus soon pulled up in front and out of it came Joya. The doctor leapt out and around to hug her in a tight embrace. They stayed that way much too long for Derek's liking, while he was stuck in his truck stewing. Finally they separated, and Dr. Benjamin got back into the driver's seat. Joya waited on the curb waving him off.

Derek was out of his truck in a flash and loping toward her. By the time Joya turned to go inside he was there.

"Whoa, you startled me," she said clutching her heart.

"I didn't want to risk getting here too late. I know you've had a long day."

She looked at him with those wide gray eyes of hers. "How long have you been waiting?" Translation, How much did you see?

"Not long."

The guard at the desk was the same woman he vaguely knew. She raised her head, acknowledging them, and then she lowered it back to her newspaper.

As they rode the elevator Derek asked, "Did you have fun tonight?"

"It was nice seeing so many people I hadn't seen in a while. Did you?"

"Those things might be a necessary evil but they bore me to death."

It was what they weren't saying, weren't asking that kept things tense.

Joya let them both in and waved him toward the sofa. "Have a seat. I'll get the quilt."

Derek sat staring out at the bay as colorful fireworks lit up the sky, kicking off the celebration. In that moment he realized he was wasting time being with any women other than Joya. Other women meant nothing to him.

He'd worked hard to put together a party and unless he wanted to attend it alone he'd better start groveling. He'd try once more to clear the air and let the chips fall where they may.

Joya had the quilt draped over her arm when she returned. She checked to make sure the dining-room table was clean before spreading the colorful fabric out.

"Is this what you had in mind?" she asked, as he got out of his seat and came closer to inspect.

Words failed him as he saw Nana Belle's one hundred years come to life in blues, yellows and reds with a little bit of green thrown in for good measure. There Nana was as a baby, and then as a young girl being taught to read by her mother. There was a portrait of her parents, a handsome man and an equally handsome dark-skinned mother.

There was a picture of Nana as a young bride when she'd married her first husband, pictures of the house as it grew, and of the children, more husbands and the arrival of grandchildren and great-grandchildren. Important events were all recorded on cloth: births, weddings, celebrations, the passages of life. There was even a picture of him. Derek wondered where Joya had gotten the photo of him in a business suit much like the one he was wearing. The work that must have gone into putting this together…the care that it took. He was choking up. He'd never met such a sensitive and sensual woman.

"Well?" she asked.

She was expecting him to say something. Anything.

"You did good. Nana is going to love it," he managed and whipped out his checkbook from inside his jacket pocket. "How much do I owe you?"

She named a figure and he squinted at her. "Come again?"

"I told you Granny and I were going to split it with you."

Derek thought about how to handle this. When they first been negotiating he'd made it clear he didn't want charity. But he didn't want to hurt Granny J's feelings either. The two old ladies were long-time friends.

He wrote out the check and handed it to Joya.

"But this is more than I told you," she said.

"It would be difficult putting a price tag on the time and care put into making an elderly woman happy. I'm sorry I've not been in touch these last few weeks. Please forgive me."

"Was there a reason?" Her concerned glance scanned his face. He saw the hurt reflected in the depths of her eyes.

He'd gotten his opening. It was time to be a brave man and step up to the plate.

"I was under the mistaken assumption that you were using me, that your only interest was in getting your grandmother's place fixed," he said, watching carefully for a change of expression.

"Who told you that?" she asked, her eyes never leaving his face.

"It's not important."

Joya approached and took his hands, her glance never wavering. "I'm not going to BS you. At first I thought you were not what I wanted. I was attracted to you but fought it every step of the way. I'm not a snob, really I'm not. My reaction was more frustration because I saw in you such potential. I brought old baggage to the situation."

"And you feel differently now that you've learned I am an educated man who just prefers working with his hands?" He had to ask and needed to know, a lot hinged on Joya's answer. He had decisions to make that might, he hoped, include her.

"I feel good that my intuition hasn't led me astray. I feel proud that a fine mind like yours hasn't been wasted. I like the complete package, both the exterior and interior. I like you," she said.

Derek held her chin in his hand, tilting her face upward until they were staring into each others eyes. "I'd hoped that you were at a point where you more than liked me. I hoped my feelings would be returned."

A spark of something flashed in her eyes. Surprise maybe? He remained on pins and needles awaiting her answer.

"Joya?"

"I care about you, Derek. It really hit home when I was at the cocktail party with someone else and you were with another woman."

"We've wasted a lot of needless time then," Derek said, kissing the top of her head. "We should remedy that."

"How so?"

"Only one way to do that, love."

He took her hand and began steering her up the hallway. She went with him, her eyes shiny with unshed tears. When he began helping her out of her dress, she did not protest.

All of Derek's pent-up feelings were released when they made love. He spent a full forty-five minutes helping her unwind, massaging her body, and kissing every exposed inch of flesh. He inhaled Joya's essence before burying himself inside her. Together they found a comfortable rhythm until, on a high, they exploded together.

"That was wonderful, love," Derek said when he slid out of her, rolled over and wrapped his arms around her. He burrowed his nose in the hollow of her shoulder. "Tell me it was good for you, too."

"Better than good," she said sleepily, yawning. "Perfect. Will you spend the night?"

"I'd love to," Derek said, a thought worrying his mind. "You mentioned earlier that the fire in your granny's place started with a cigarette but neither of you smoke."

"You would have to bring that up," she grumbled.

"I was trying my best to forget about it." She yawned again.

"All of your sales help smoke. Could be one of them."

"Ex sales help you mean. And no, I didn't know they smoked." He could tell from her voice she was wide awake and alert. "And you're thinking that it might be…"

"Current sales help smokes, too. When I was working on the shops next to yours they'd congregate out back and have a cigarette with my guys."

"All of them?"

"Every last one of them."

"And by chance do you know what kind of cigarettes they smoked?"

He thought about it for a moment.

"All I remember was a green-and-white pack. I remember on several occasions they tried to get me to join them."

"This may be a good lead. I'll call Lionel and Greg tomorrow," Joya said, excited although she stifled another yawn. "Right now, I just want you to hold me."

And he did. In Derek's mind he was holding Joya forever.

Chapter 20

Joya awoke for the second time that morning to find it pouring outside. She'd made love to Derek earlier as the rain pelted against the window panes and the waves crashed against rocks. He'd left right before dawn, citing a long day ahead of him. He'd wanted to get an early start with the preparations for Nana Belle's birthday. And he'd been worried, because if the rain didn't stop the rented party tent would be too small.

Realizing she would be late, Joya poured coffee into her travel mug and grabbed an umbrella. Taking the cup with her, she drove like a mad person to the store. Granny J already had the shutters up and was waiting on her first customers. Any conversation was tabled until the customers completed their transactions and left.

"Did you have a good time with Dr. Ben?" Granny J asked the moment they were out of sight.

"He is very attentive."

Gran raised an eyebrow and waited. "That's it? No chemistry, as you young people say?"

Time to change the topic. "Did you know your sales people smoked?" Joya asked.

Gran shrugged. "As long as I'm not inhaling their smoke, what's it to me?"

"I'm about to call Lionel and Greg just to be sure they know, too." Joya added.

Granny J sucked her teeth. "You would think they would already know that much. I've called the insurance company. They're going to send an inspector out."

"Well, we'll just close the door until the inspector shows up and does his assessment."

"Okay by me. The burning smell's almost gone. I opened all the windows."

Still euphoric over how last evening had ended, Joya went off to call Greg. She was fortunate enough to find him at the precinct and shared with him what Derek had told her.

"We've spoken with LaTisha and Deborah," he said. "They have alibis and we've talked to the people they were with." He sounded complacent. That irritated her.

"What about Portia?"

"She was interviewed during the quilt incident and came up clean. We can talk to her again. I'll get back to you," Greg said before hanging up.

Joya returned to the outer room to find several customers browsing. On the verandah, another group was going through the centennial quilts, oohing and aahhing. If business continued like this they might have to stay open later than usual.

Joya had asked Portia to come in, so that she and Granny J could leave at a reasonable time to get ready for Nana Belle's party. Now that she and Derek had resolved their situation, she was excited about attending, and couldn't wait to see the elderly woman's reaction when she got her first glimpse of that quilt.

"Phone for you," Granny J said, handing her the new portable. "Last evening must have gone better than you thought." There was a twinkle in the old lady's eye, a glimmer of hope.

Joya stabbed her index finger in the air. "Don't you dare start up, hear? Hey sweetie, I missed you," she said into the mouthpiece.

"That's a reassuring greeting and most unexpected. How are you?" Kyle Benjamin said.

Disappointment washed over her. His was not the voice Joya wanted to hear.

"I couldn't be better. Things are a bit busy here, but busy means money so we'll take it."

"I had a very good time last evening. You're excellent company," Kyle said.

"Thank you and so are you."

"I realize this is late notice but would you consider attending tomorrow's unveiling of the bronze flamingo; the one given to us by the President to commemorate the city's hundredth anniversary? The ceremony takes place in the town square and there's a luncheon afterward. I would be delighted if you went with me."

She would have to turn him down diplomatically.

"It's very nice of you to ask," Joya said, "but I'm afraid I have to say no. I've agreed to attend most of the festivities with someone else. Thanks for thinking of me though."

"What a lucky man he is. Should something change, please give me a call."

Granny J had been shamelessly eavesdropping.

"You let him down nicely," she said.

"Gran, Kyle Benjamin is a nice man but it's just not happening here." Joya tapped her heart. "I already know that and I don't want to mislead him."

"It's Derek, isn't it?"

Joya nodded. "He makes me feel like a princess. He makes me feel so loved."

"Nothing wrong with following your heart," her grandmother said wisely.

Age and experience talking, perhaps it was time to listen. She'd already had a failed marriage and a couple of hard knocks. It had taken all that to make her realize that what you saw wasn't always what you got.

The phone rang. Thinking it was Derek, Joya grabbed it up. "Are you sitting down?" Greg asked.

"Should I be?"

"We've apprehended a suspect and we're bringing others in."

"Anyone I know?"

Greg cleared his throat and Joya prepared herself for whatever was coming.

"Your employee, Portia, broke when we told her we'd found a cigarette stub the same kind as she smoked. Of course, we were bluffing since we didn't know her brand. She began spilling the beans before we could even read her her rights."

"That sweet little girl who was going off to college was responsible?" Joya asked in shock.

"Not so sweet, she was in collusion with the other two employees, the ones you fired. They got one of their gang-member friends to break the window as a warning to you. But it was Portia who left that window open so the same thug could enter the store and vandalize it. And it was Portia who intentionally dropped that lit cigarette in the stock room. The others dared her. She was so desperate to be liked by that bunch of losers that she followed through."

"Maybe I will sit down," Joya said, sitting heavily. "I'm having a hard time processing this information."

Greg continued, telling her what she needed to do to prosecute the suspects. Joya's head was spinning by the time she hung up. Wait until she told Derek about this latest development. But first she had to let Granny J know what had happened. It was her store after all. She hoped her gran would not be too devastated by the turn of events.

"Do what you need to do," Granny J said, her eyes moist when she'd heard the story.

"I will as long as you're okay with it. I propose we close up shop and head home. We have a long night ahead of us."

"And to think I was helping pay that child's tuition," Granny J said, dabbing at her eyes with a hankie.

So that was another reason her grandmother had taken out an equity loan. What an ungrateful piece of work that child was.

Joya took her grandmother by the arm. "We'll party hearty tonight in celebration of those good-for-nothings being caught."

Granny J remained silent. She was already busy pulling cash from the register and bustling around the store to close. Joya had to admire the older woman's resilience, but then again she'd probably seen everything and heard everything twice. It was she who was a true survivor.

Hours later, feeling refreshed from a nap and a long shower, Joya swung by Granny J's house to pick her up. Gran was standing out on her little porch, looking pretty in a champagne-colored silk pantsuit and a jaunty hat. A feather in the hatband fluttered in the breeze. Joya thought she looked especially festive, rested and in the mood to celebrate her friend's birthday.

Needing a pick-me-up, Joya had splurged on her way home, stopping to buy a dress from one of the new boutiques. She'd spent way too much money, but she wanted to look especially nice for Derek. And she wanted to reward herself. It had been one tough week.

"Ready to go, Gran?" she called as she climbed from the driver's seat.

"No need to come get me, I'm not some old lady that needs a helping hand. My ankle is all healed and my heart's on the mend, thank you," Granny said, coming down the two little steps with a bounce to her walk and sliding into the front seat of Joya's sporty car. "Maybe we can take the top down and arrive in style."

Joya pushed a button and the convertible roof slid back. A balmy breeze cooled them instantly. Granny J grabbed her hat so it wouldn't blow away.

The going was tedious as they meandered through congested streets, slowing to watch the action. On this second day of the centennial celebrations, pedestrians were out in full force. Clowns juggled and performed outrageous antics on the sidewalk, musicians strummed instruments and artists painted caricatures of tourists. Costumed entertainers roamed and panhandled.

Finally they arrived at Nana Belle's house, although initially Joya whizzed past. It didn't look a thing like the house she remembered, gone was the white façade and the decks that went off in crazy directions.

This house was painted coral and the deck railings and trim were a complementary beige color. There were huge window walls instead of old crank-out windows, and there were silver balloons and a huge sign that said Party Within.

She'd never seen so many people in her life. They filled the decks and overflowed the porch. In the front yard, people sat on folding chairs sipping from little paper cups. And laughter and music came from the area where a decorated white tent had been erected.

"I'll drop you off here, Gran, and be right back," Joya said, temporarily double parking because there was no choice.

"You're treating me like an old lady again," Granny J groused.

"You *are* an old lady," Joya teased the woman she loved even more than Derek, but in an entirely different way.

Granny J made a face and got out. Joya waited until her grandmother was inside the yard before moving off. She followed the signs for the huge public outdoor lot where beach traffic normally parked during the day. To her surprise and amazement, white-clad attendants waving flashlights beckoned her in. Derek had cleared it with the city to take over the lot. After circling a couple of times she found a spot.

If she'd anticipated such a far walk she would never have worn heels. What to do now? Both a golf cart and jitney with striped awning pulled up at the same time. Joya gratefully sank into the golf cart and was whizzed away in style to the party.

Derek waited out front and she felt her stomach flutter and her palms grow damp. Just the sight of him made her want to jump his bones. He came over to help her out and planted a kiss on her lips, complete with plenty of tongue.

"Your grandmother told me you were parking. I thought, rather than you having to find me I'd come meet you."

"You think of everything." She stood on tiptoes to wrap her arms around his neck.

Another kiss followed. Joya could feel the eyes boring into their backs. Who cared? Eventually they separated. He twined his fingers through hers and started guiding her inside. "How about I get the cake and gifts out of the way before Nana gets tired? If she slips away quietly, bet you anything this crowd continues to party."

"Good plan. I'd like to say hello anyway, and wish her happy birthday in private. Perhaps we can give Nana our joint gift now. It would be nice to share her history as the other gifts are being opened. I'll help you hang the quilt on the wall behind her. Not many of us will live to be one hundred."

"You and I will," Derek said, sneaking another kiss before he led the way inside. Joya didn't dare hope. She'd accept it for what it was.

Delicious smells came at her when Derek stopped by the kitchen to give the catering staff a heads-up. He wanted cake and champagne to be brought out in fifteen minutes.

At last they left to find Nana Belle.

The centenarian was seated in the great room on a chair that had been specially made for the occasion. She gazed out to sea, smoking her usual cigarette. Her throne was covered with a satin slipcover, the type tied with a bow. It had glitter sprinkled all over.

At her feet were her senior citizen friends. Occasionally she bobbed a wobbly tiara at them to let them know she was listening.

Granny J and Ida Rosenstein who lived at Flamingo Place toasted her from little paper cups which they kept sipping on. Joya strongly suspected those cups held scotch.

Joya greeted the centenarian while Derek headed off to get their gift. Soon he returned with the quilt on a hanger. Where he'd found the gigantic ribbon and bow he'd wrapped the quilt in was anyone's guess.

"What you got there, boy?" Nana Belle asked, lighting up yet another cigarette, which none of her buddies seemed to mind.

"A gift from me, Granny J and Joya," Derek said, taking the cigarette from her and passing it to one of the guests to put out.

"Oh!" She sounded pleased.

Derek, with the help of Granny J, unfolded the quilt and placed it on Nana Belle's lap. Her fingers were too arthritic to maneuver the material so they smoothed it out, holding up some of the blocks. She wheezed loudly and her rheumy old eyes filled with tears. Joya feared she might have a heart attack.

"Where did you find these pictures, boy?" she asked when she could catch her breath. She slowly examined the quilt, while others read the messages that her guests had written with a special pen.

"I have my ways," he said, beaming, clearly pleased by his great-grandmother's reaction.

"Do you like your gift, Nana Belle?" Joya asked, cautiously. So much love and patience had gone into it. Even with additional help and everyone pulling together, it had taken many, many hours to tell the story of Nana Belle's life.

"It's a dream, something to be cherished for the rest of my life. There's another gift that I'd like though," the old lady said slyly.

"You name it, Nana." Derek was accommodating as always. Joya could tell he loved the old lady dearly, just like she loved her Granny J.

Nana paused for dramatic effect and began wheezing again. Joya's own heart almost stopped. "Before your old nana goes I want to see you married and settled."

Oh, boy! Talk about putting them on the spot.

Derek wrapped his arms around Joya and brought her up against him. "First, I have a couple of important decisions to make." He kissed Joya's forehead. "A lot depends on the lady I love whether I return to Chicago and the corporate grind or whether I make

Flamingo Beach home. I've been offered a partnership here with Rowan James."

Joya clapped a hand to her mouth. "Oh, Derek, that's wonderful."

Derek was trusting her to help him make the right decision. They'd need to have a little talk in private, maybe later after the cake. She'd thought she loved life in a big city, but there was something to be said for a growing beach community like Flamingo Beach.

Now that Granny J was back on her feet, Joya was free to pursue the events-planning job Emilie had mentioned. Derek had already done the corporate thing and decided it wasn't for him, and she couldn't imagine any amount of money would make him love it any more. Their families were here: the people they loved. Nosey as some of them could be.

The lights above Nana Belle's head dimmed and flashed. People began coming in from outside, crowding the room. Joya spotted the projection screens up above. Derek had thought of everything. Those who weren't able to get up that close would see the event on the plasma TVs.

On screen, a local television reporter was talking to Tre Monroe about his interview with Nana Belle and excerpts could be heard over the noise of the guests. A path was soon cleared and a huge cake was wheeled into the center of the room.

Derek took that moment to whisper in her ear, "I'll be planning an event just like this one for you. If you can stand being around me for sixty-plus years."

Joya looked at him with her heart in her eyes. She gave his hand a little squeeze.

"I could be with you forever and ever," she said, meaning it. She shouted over the noise, "Happy Birthday, Nana Belle. You got your other present!"

The old lady stood and took a couple of faltering steps. The room hushed. "Thank you, Lord," she said.

"Speech! Speech!" the attendees chanted.

"Sheesh, no speech from me. I'd have too much to say." Faltering at times, Nana Belle blew out the flickering flames that spelled out one hundred in several breaths.

"Happy Birthday to me," Belle sang. "Happy Birthday Flamingo Beach! I never would have thought we'd make it a full century."

As more applause broke out around them, Derek whispered into Joya's ear, "I love you, Joya Hamill. This century and the next."

tangled ROOTS

A Kendra Clayton Novel

ANGELA HENRY

Nothing's going right these days for part-time English teacher and reluctant sleuth Kendra Clayton. Now her favorite student is the number one suspect in a local murder. When he begs Kendra for help, she's soon on the road to trouble again—trying to find the real killer, stepping into danger...and getting tangled in the deadly roots of desire.

"This debut mystery features an exciting new African-American heroine.... Highly recommended."
—*Library Journal* on *The Company You Keep*

Available the first week of May wherever books are sold.

KIMANI PRESS™

www.kimanipress.com

KPAH0680507